A Singular Mission
An Olympia Brown Mystery

by

Judith Campbell

Mainly Murder Press, LLC
PO Box 290586
Wethersfield, CT 06129-0586
www.mainlymurderpress.com

Mainly Murder Press

Copy Editor: Paula Knudson
Executive Editor: Judith K. Ivie
Cover Designer: Karen A. Phillips

All rights reserved

Copyright © 2014 by Judith Campbell
Paperback ISBN 978-0-9913628-6-8
Ebook ISBN 978-0-9905103-2-1

Published in the United States of America by

Mainly Murder Press, LLC
PO Box 290586
Wethersfield, CT 06129-0586
www.MainlyMurderPress.com

Dedication

To our grandchildren, Leah, Anna, Melissa, Spencer and Erica. You put stars in our eyes, joy in our hearts and give us hope for the future—and to their parents, Ian and Liz, Colin and Laura, thank you. It just doesn't get any better.

~

Acknowledgments

No author works alone, and no book gets to be published without the help and support of friends, colleagues and family. First last and always, thank you to my Professional Englishman, husband, best friend and "alpha reader," Chris Stokes (AKA Frederick Watkins).

To the Spirited Writers in the UK, the 3 on 3 Writers in Kingston, Massachusetts, and the OBPL writers on Martha's Vineyard, thank you for listening, commenting, challenging me and, most of all, being honest. To my readers who are so very supportive and encouraging—and, I might lovingly add, are becoming a bunch of much beloved nags—I say thank you from the bottom of my heart and the end of my pen! I am so encouraged by you all.

Praise for the Olympia Brown Mysteries

"In *A Predatory Mission,* author and minister, the Reverend Dr. Judith Campbell takes on the highly charged subject of clergy sex abuse. She writes honestly and clearly about this much talked about but poorly understood subject. She does not back away from the truth or the untoward and illustrates plainly how a predator sexually assaults those whom he was called to pastor. I have added Campbell's book as required reading, next to those of Nathaniel Hawthorne, John Updike and Sinclair Lewis, in the courses and programs I offer on clergy sexual misconduct. Like Hawthorne in *The Scarlet Letter,* Campbell writes about the real and serious damage done to people by clergy hypocrisy and abuse of power. But unlike Hawthorne, her novel is accessible and entertaining. You will not be able to put it down."

The Reverend Dr. Deborah J. Pope-Lance, minister, psychotherapist and consultant on clergy malpractice and creating safe congregations

"*An Unspeakable Mission* is an engaging and thought-provoking story of two dedicated and impassioned clerics struggling to find the truth when secrets and silence are the expected norms. And when 21st century religion gets involved with religious and cultural expectations of the past, the story doesn't always turn out as expected. I kept turning the pages to see what would happen next."

Rev. Keith Kron, Director of the Transitions Office for the Unitarian Universalist Association

"Judith Campbell does a superb job in the follow-up to her suspense/thriller, *A Deadly Mission,* as Olympia Brown is once again tangled up in the personal life of one of her students, an ugly secret too horrible to speak of, and a death that looks suspiciously like murder!"

Brenda Scott, Manchester Contemporary Literary Examiner, Examiner.com

"Rev. Judith Campbell has done it again in *An Unspeakable Mission,* her second in the Olympia Brown mystery series. Using her experience as an ordained minister as well as a writer, Judith deftly weaves a compelling mystery about the death of an abusive alcoholic in a suspicious house fire, with the horrific subjects of incest and domestic violence. …a perfect balance between building suspense and giving voice to victims who can't speak for themselves, proving in the process that what often seems obvious ... isn't."

Dawn Braash, avid reader and owner of Bunch of Grapes, the flagship bookstore of Martha's Vineyard where authors and readers find everything they are looking for.

The Olympia Brown "Mission Mystery" Series
(in order of publication)

A Deadly Mission
An Unspeakable Mission
A Despicable Mission
An Unholy Mission
A Predatory Mission
An Improper English Mission
A Singular Mission

Prologue

Rev. Olympia Brown didn't see the Valentine's Day gift bag hanging on the back of the door until she was seated at her desk in the church office. Cheery pink and red tissue paper was spilling out of the top, and a tangle of curly ribbons twirled and tumbled down the sides. She grimaced and bit her lip.

It would likely be some sort of little trinket or useless knick-knack, the kind she particularly loathed—a statue of a sad-eyed kid in a nightgown or one more goddamn angel with a sappy message about how God is watching over you etched into the bottom. Only it wasn't God watching over her. It was a woman named Emily Goodale who, from the day Olympia started a three month contract at the Salt Rock Fellowship, had attached herself to Olympia like a homeless kitten.

Seeing it hanging there, she recalled a warning from her days in seminary. The Pastoral Ministry Professor had looked over her glasses at the ministers in training and said, "Watch out for the note takers and the gift givers. You need to handle them with kid gloves, and at the same time you need to watch your back. They can spell trouble."

"Damn," said Olympia, half in defeat and half in resignation, "I thought I'd taken care of this."

"Are you talking to me?" called a voice from the next room. It was Charlotte Herlihy, the church administrator, who had ears like a hawk has eyes.

"No, just thinking out loud. Do I have any appointments this afternoon? There's something I need to sort out, and it can't wait."

"Clear on this end," came the disembodied voice. "Anything I can help with? I can stay on, if you want."

"I only wish there were." Olympia grumbled under her breath. "No, thanks, Charlotte, I'm good."

"Well, don't stay too late. You don't want to get stuck down here once that storm gets going. We don't usually get too much snow on the Cape, but every once in a while we get totally hammered."

"I hear you. My mother always said, 'Better safe than sorry.' That's why we came in early, remember? So we could beat the storm. Do you know when it's supposed to start?"

"The TV weather lady said it would probably begin in the early afternoon. It's supposed to be nasty, rain turning to ice, then turning to snow. They're talking about power outages and dangerous road conditions, the whole works. Come to think of it, they've already declared a state of emergency starting at two this afternoon, but we'll be safely home by then."

Wonderful, thought Olympia. With a sense of irritation and foreboding, she got up from her desk and retrieved the gift. Under the gaily colored tissue was a crushed dead rose, its stem snapped in two, and an unsigned children's penny valentine bearing the word, "Forever."

Until the previous Saturday night, only four days ago, Emily had seemed to be nothing more than a lonely, insecure woman who came to church looking for someone to befriend her. Now Olympia knew differently. She got up and walked into the next room to where the Office Administrator was sitting. She was a good-looking no-nonsense woman, likely in her sixties, who favored color coordinated slacks and tailored shirts over girlie frills and ruffles. Today she was dressed in shades of beige and tan.

"Hey, Charlotte, by any chance did Emily Goodale come in here this morning?"

"Not that I know of. I've been here since eight, and I unlocked the place."

Then how and when did this latest little unwelcome gift get in here? Olympia bit her lip and reached for her phone. She didn't have much time. This particular storm was bearing down on everyone.

One

January 25, 1863

Bitterly cold again today—merely going outside for a few logs for the fire chills me to the bone. Sammy, the cat, and my darling Jonathan are quite restive with being indoors for so long, and I must confess my patience is getting a bit thin. I am concerned for the birds and the little animals in weather like this. I do put bits of bread and table scraps out for the birds, and it all disappears so I do take some measure of comfort in that. Jonathan keeps himself busy chasing after Sammy and learning new words now, more and more every day to the delight of us all.

Aunt Louisa is content to sit by the fire and read or knit and, more often, doze. I fear she is beginning to show her age, but I shall never be the one to mention it. Richard, my husband in name only and my friend for life, has noticed this, as well. Perhaps she will stay on with me now and not go back to Cambridge where there is no one to look after her. I shall suggest it ... carefully!

Most nights Richard takes his evening meal with us, and just as often as not, he prepares it. He is fond of cooking and quite accomplished with it, as well. I do not complain, for in truth it is most agreeable. Domesticity is not one of my strong points. It is a very equitable arrangement we all would appear to have achieved. Richard has a family who loves him for who he is. Jonathan has a father of sorts. I have a dear friend. Aunt Louisa has people to attend her and people she can knit for. She likes to keep busy, but she does tire easily. She assures me she's feeling well enough, but nonetheless, I am concerned.

More Anon, LFW

Olympia Brown set the leather bound diary down on the table beside her chair and thought back to the day she had accepted the position of supply minister for the Salt Rock Chapel. It was a picturebook white, steepled church on upper Cape Cod, the minister of which would be on sabbatical for three months. They told her they were looking for someone to preach on Sundays and be available for pastoral care—in other words, hold the place together until the regular pastor returned. The appointment was to begin on the fifteenth of January and continue through the ides of April, just three months. She would be little more than a place holder with a clerical collar and provider of the weekly sermon.

In the telephone interview Catherine Allen, the board president, had said it would be a piece of cake she could do with her eyes shut.

Olympia had been told a similar story once before. That time, she'd landed on Martha's Vineyard with the business end of a gun pointed in her direction.

She remembered the very first time she'd ever heard mention of Salt Rock. It had been an unseasonably warm day shortly after Christmas, and she'd been sitting in the office of district supervisor, Zak Bilecki. He was eager for her to take the position, and she was lifting a skeptical eyebrow in his direction.

"Why don't you tell me the whole story, Zak? Nothing is ever that simple in this line of work."

"There isn't one that I know of." He smiled and held out both hands in the Come to Jesus gesture. "Look at it this way; it's a great opportunity for you to enjoy a short ministry in a healthy, family-sized church in a charming location. You'll make a little money, and they'll have a minister they can count on."

"In the dead of winter," she added.

"But the Cape never gets as much snow as the other side of the bridge," he wheedled.

"I know, except when it does, and then it always melts in a day or two. Tell me more. You need to convince me."

In the end he'd accomplished his mission. Olympia signed the contract, agreeing to begin work in mid-January, just two weeks after the start of the New Year. Within days of that she got a phone call from a woman in the congregation.

"Hi, is this Reverend Brown? My name is Emily Goodale. I'm a member of Salt Rock. I just wanted to call and say welcome to the Fellowship on behalf of all of us and tell you how happy we are to have a woman in the pulpit for a change."

"Why, thank you, Emily. It's very kind of you. Do be sure to introduce yourself to me so I won't feel like such a stranger on that first day. Um, was there anything else you wanted to talk about?"

Olympia was absent-mindedly stroking her sleek black cat Cadeau, who had stretched himself out in a patch of winter sunlight on her desk next to the computer.

"Oh, no—well, not right now anyway, Reverend—but it's sweet of you to ask. They said you were friendly and easy to talk to, and I guess you really are. I volunteered to be one of the ushers on your first Sunday so I'll be there to help introduce you to the congregation. I believe it's important to make a new person feel welcome, don't you?"

"It's very thoughtful of you to be so considerate."

"I'm really looking forward to meeting you. Goodbye, Reverend."

"See you in a few weeks, Emily. 'Bye now."

Olympia should have paid more attention to what it had been about the conversation that made her feel uncomfortable. She really should have, because if she had, things might have gone very differently.

Two weeks after that she started work at the church on the Wednesday before her first Sunday in the pulpit. She wanted to have a few days on site to acquaint herself with the building and the community before actually standing up in front of them. She had just settled into the chair behind the massive old mahogany desk in her office when a woman, wrapped in bulky winter clothing, walked into the office holding out a cup of coffee.

"Hi, Reverend. I'm Emily Goodale, remember me? I called you a couple of weeks ago. I'm a member here. Well, I was on my way to the grocery store, and I stopped for a coffee and decided to get one for you, too. You don't mind, do you?"

There was no possible answer to that other than, "Of course not, it was very thoughtful. Thank you." Olympia really did like coffee, and this was fresh and hot. She pushed away the twice-nuked stuff she'd brought from home and reached for the steaming cardboard container.

"Um, Reverend?"

"Yes, Emily?"

"Could I make an appointment to talk with you sometime? There are some things I probably should talk about with someone, but I never felt comfortable with Reverend Rutledge. Maybe it's because he's a man, but he never acted as though he really cared about what I had to say. You're different. I could tell that when I called you back in December."

Olympia scrambled around in the recesses of her brain trying to recall the phone call.

"Don't you remember?" Emily was looking both hurt and anxious.

"Of course I remember. It's just that I spoke to a lot of people from the church that week, and I don't know anyone's face yet. Now I know at least one. Mmm, exactly when were you thinking?"

Still frowning, Emily began to unbutton her coat. "Well, I'm here right now, and I've got a few minutes, so I thought maybe …"

Olympia pulled a datebook out of her handbag and set it on her desk. "If this isn't a spiritual emergency, Emily, I'd like to wait to meet with anyone until after I've done my first Sunday service. I have some time next Tuesday at eleven. Would that work for you? It's less than a week from today."

Emily looked crestfallen. "I really hoped … I mean, it won't take very long, but I suppose if you're busy …" She undid another button and waited for Olympia to relent and invite her to sit down.

"Probably not a good idea. You see, I've left this morning open for drop-ins, and it sounds as though this might be need to be a longer and more private conversation. I'm afraid we'd be interrupted today, and that wouldn't be fair to you. I want to be able to give you my full attention."

"You do?" The wary and petulant frown vanished, and suddenly she was all smiles once again.

"So next week, Tuesday at eleven?"

"Gee, I don't have my calendar with me, but can I call and let you know?"

"You can leave a message on the church phone. I'll be sure to check it."

"I could call you at home." A hopeful smile.

"I'd rather you called here. That way I'll be sure to get it. My husband isn't the best of message takers."

"I'll try, Reverend; it depends on when I get home. So you're married?"

Olympia smiled and nodded. "Just make sure you let me know one way or the other, okay?"

"Sure, Reverend, and if there's anything you need help with, just give me a call. I think it's important to support the minister." She lowered her voice. "Not everyone here does, so be careful, and you didn't hear me say that."

"Thank you, Emily."

When she left, Olympia sat staring at the door and shaking her head. Poor thing, she thought. She'd encountered her kind before, pathetically in need of attention and approval from the person in charge—the teacher, the parent, the coach—and in this case, the minister. The trick was finding the right balance, enough attention and affirmation to let her know she was a valued member of the community, but not so much that she formed an unhealthy attachment, or others felt excluded. Balance and boundaries were the key words here, and Olympia was very familiar with them. Easy to say, not so easy to maintain. She knew that, too.

"Reverend?"

Olympia looked up.

Emily was back.

"There's something I forgot to say."

"What's that?"

"I'm bringing the pulpit flowers for Sunday. What's your favorite color?"

Two

Olympia's first Sunday service was pretty much standard issue as far as the format was concerned. Her colleagues would have called it a typical three-hymn sandwich with the sermon, the collection and maybe an anthem for the filling. She'd chosen a rather subdued blue-grey pantsuit, which set off her deep rose clerical shirt and shiny white plastic collar to perfection. Over this she arranged a brightly colored stole to complete the ensemble. First impressions counted for a lot. A little dignity brightened with a splash of color that said "professional but not drab." It was exactly how Olympia, a mid-life woman of comfortable proportions, liked to present herself. She had never been blessed with the svelte figure of a Vogue model, and being well into her fifties, she was content with the status quo. A few well-placed grey hairs, a couple of smile lines and bright green eyes completed the picture she presented to the world. She wore practical clothing, comfortable shoes and a wash-and-wear hairstyle that required nothing more than a hot shower and a dollar bottle of shampoo to make it look decent. On that first morning she'd done all that could be done, and she was ready to take on her new assignment.

The service was well attended for a cold Sunday in mid-January, and she was pleased and surprised to see that the straight-backed white pews were almost full, and the people sitting in them were mostly smiling. She was duly introduced to everyone by the president of the board with a broadly smiling Emily standing at attention right beside her. The three hymns were relatively familiar, and nobody snored during the sermon. Add to that, several people made favorable comments when she greeted them at the back of the church as they made their way to the social hour.

So far so good, she told herself as she walked back down the center aisle toward the pulpit. She needed to retrieve her notes and her hymnbook before going back to the parish hall for a well-earned cup of coffee and maybe a cookie or three.

It was only when she turned back that she saw the young woman, well wrapped in winter clothing, sitting alone in the last pew. Olympia didn't remember seeing her during the service. When had she come in? On the other hand, with so many people there that morning, it was possible she simply hadn't noticed.

Olympia fixed a welcoming smile on her face and extended her hand as she approached the woman.

"Good morning. I'm Reverend Olympia Brown. This is my first Sunday here, so I don't know too many people yet. Are you a member of the congregation?"

The woman shook her head.

Olympia slipped into the pew and sat down beside her. "So this your first time here too? Well, then, welcome to Salt Rock. What's your name?"

The young woman spoke in a voice that was little more than a whisper.

"I'm Eileen Sullivan. I don't go to this church. I go to Our Lady of the Sea on the lower Cape. I'm a Catholic, but I came here because, well, I need to talk to someone. I heard there was a new lady minister here. I took a chance. I don't know much about Protestant churches, so I hope I'm not doing the wrong thing."

This was not what Olympia wanted to hear. She wanted a cup of coffee, and after that she wanted to go home to

Frederick and the cats. But the look in the woman's eyes and the tension that was literally radiating from her body told her that whatever this was, it needed attention right this minute.

Olympia turned more fully towards the woman.

"Can you tell me what's troubling you?"

Eileen stared at the floor, and Olympia waited in gentle silence. Finally Eileen began to speak.

"I'm not sure what to say or how to say it except that something's happened, and I don't have much time, and I simply don't know what to do or where to go for help. It took everything I have in me to walk in here."

Olympia spoke softly. "Take your time. I'm not going anywhere."

Before Eileen could respond a door creaked open at the back of the church, and a cheery voice called out.

"Reverend Olympia! There you are. Will you be coming in for coffee?"

Olympia turned to see Catherine Allen, the slender and stylish president of the board, breezing toward them. "Everybody wants to meet you. Oh, I'm sorry. Is this a private conversation?"

It was until now, thought Olympia with more than a little irritation. Say as little as possible.

"Not really private, just a quick check-in with a first time visitor. I'll be there in a couple of minutes. Save me something yummy, will you?"

Catherine laughed and patted her totally flat stomach. "Of course. I'll make up a plate and set it near the microwave. See you in a few."

When she was gone Eileen Sullivan started to get up, but then she changed her mind and dropped back down onto the wooden pew.

"I really should go. I have no business just walking into a strange place and dumping my problems on a woman who doesn't know me from Adam. I'm sorry."

Olympia held up her hand. "This isn't a strange place, it's a church, and it's exactly where you should come if something is bothering you. It is, however, not the best time for either of us. I need to be able to give you my full attention, and right now there are fifty or sixty people out in the parish hall waiting to have coffee with me. Would it be possible for you to come back in an hour and talk with me in my office? That way we won't be rushed or disturbed."

Eileen nodded, and this time she did get up. "Thank you, Reverend. This is very kind of you. Um, where's your office?"

Olympia waved her hand off to the right. "There's a door around to the side, the cemetery side, that is. I have my own personal entrance … or exit. I don't expect too many people use it in the winter. Usually people enter through the main door of the church and come in through the social hall. If you use the side door, no one will see you. I'll be waiting."

Eileen Sullivan did her best to smile as she buttoned up her coat. She gave it a little tug and smoothed it over her hips and stomach. Then she looped a bright green knitted scarf around her neck and, without another word, turned and slipped out of the church.

Olympia remained sitting in the wooden pew, rubbing her temples. She had a pretty good idea of what the problem might be—and if her womanly instinct was correct, and it usually was, then what? She'd been in a similar position herself many years ago, and knew just exactly how terrified and alone the young woman was feeling. "Help me, Jesus," she whispered into the empty space around her.

"Reverend?"

Catherine Allen was back.

Olympia blinked and smiled, and then she stood.

"Here I come, ready or not. Now lead me to your coffee pot."

When in doubt, crack a joke, she thought. Sometimes it even worked.

The church social hour was a noisy mix of happy people enjoying themselves and the company of one another. The aroma of fresh coffee wafted over the chatter, and the combined scents of cinnamon, lemon and chocolate drew Olympia right into the middle of it all. She followed her nose to the coffee pot and from there on to the food table, where she spotted the plate of sweets Catherine had prepared for her. Thus armed, with a mug in one hand and the plate in the other, she began making the circuit of the sun-filled room. Most of the people were wearing name tags, so conversation was comfortable and almost familiar. This was good. Here was a church community dressed in their Sunday best, greeting one another, doing bits of church business and welcoming and embracing the stranger.

In an hour they would all be gone, the church kitchen would be wiped down, and she would be sitting in her office trying to comfort a very troubled young woman. She would be the one welcoming and embracing the stranger. Olympia made a mental note to call Frederick and tell him she'd be late.

"Reverend?" The voice was a familiar one.

"Oh, hi, Emily. Happy Sunday morning to you." The woman was wearing one of those oversized down parkas that made her look a little bit like a marshmallow on stilts.

"Thank you. I just wanted to say what a good service that was. I really enjoyed the sermon."

Olympia took an unconscious step backward. "It's very kind of you to say so."

"Can I get you another cookie or top up your coffee?" Emily managed to look simultaneously anxious and hopeful.

"You are too kind, but I haven't even finished what I have here. Thanks all the same."

"So, we're still on for Tuesday?"

"Unless you've changed your mind, we are," said Olympia.

"Oh, no, I was just checking."

"Always a good idea, but let's save any more conversation for then. I don't want to rush you off, but we'll have our very own time in a couple of days, and I really do need to get to know names and faces while I have the opportunity."

"Oh, sorry, I didn't mean to keep you."

Olympia did not grit her teeth, but she wanted to. Instead, she said, "You're hardly keeping me, Emily. We ministers work on Sundays, and that includes the coffee hour. That's when we try and at least check in with everyone. Some people think we only work for twenty minutes a week, but I usually try and stay for the whole morning."

The humor was lost on Emily, who nodded in solemn agreement and then started off toward the food table.

Olympia looked around the room, trying to decide who she should talk to next, and spotted an impeccably dressed older gentleman sitting off by himself near the kitchen. She polished off another cookie on the way and took the seat next to him. Before speaking she glanced down at his name tag. "Good morning, Forrest, I'm Olympia Brown. I'll be here for the next three months, and I'm trying to learn people's names. Thank you for coming this morning."

The white haired, bespectacled gentleman squinted in her direction and said, "Huh? You'll have to speak up, I'm deaf, and you're sitting on my bad side."

Olympia moved around to his good side and tried again, this time speaking more loudly and using fewer words.

That worked. He responded, "Pleased to meet you. I've been coming to this church for eighty years, and I've seen a lot of ministers come and go through these doors." Then he leaned closer and lowered his voice. "Tell me, how old do you think I am?"

Olympia gulped and decided to play it safe. "Eighty-five?" she hollered.

The man rocked back in his chair with smug grin. It was clear he'd played this game before. "I'm ninety-four. Moved here when I was seven. I can tell you stories of things that happened here before you were born, Missy."

Olympia looked dutifully amazed and thought, I'll bet you can, but you're not going to do it right now. She said, "And I'm going to hold you to it, but not today. As I said, I'm trying to learn names."

"Huh?"

"How about next week?" she yelled.

"Best offer I've had all year," he cackled.

Olympia stifled a laugh, wished him well and set off to meet and greet her way around the hall via the sweets table. After all, a working woman needs to keep up her strength.

For the next forty-five minutes Olympia circulated, greeting the adults, admiring babies and dodging the Sunday School kids as they galloped around the perimeter of the hall. She was enjoying herself. Meeting new people in a lovely old church on a bright winter morning was one of the unspoken perks of her curious profession, and these were lovely folks. Church congregations had personalities. Some approached the stranger with polite caution, others were carefully curious. Some were overwhelming and almost aggressively friendly, trying to convince the first-time visitor to join on the spot. This was going to be an easy group. Salt Rock was in a tourist area. These people were used to a steady flow of one-time visitors, as well as the more predictable comings and goings of the familiar seasonal visitors who came regularly and stayed in their nearby vacation homes.

By 12:30 the hall was empty, and the kitchen ladies were putting away the last of the cups and saucers and deciding which of them would take home the leftovers.

"Hey, Reverend Olympia!" Jocelyn Carver was waving and beckoning through the service window to the kitchen. "You want to take some of this stuff home? We usually just divide it up unless there's an AA meeting or something; then we might want to leave it for them. There's more than enough to go around."

"You don't have to twist my arm, Jocelyn. You've got some excellent cooks in this church. I won't have to make dessert tonight. My husband will be thrilled. He's got a bit of a sweet tooth."

Jocelyn grinned, held out a foil-covered plate and winked. "Just make sure it gets home okay."

"Was I that obvious?" asked Olympia with a sheepish grin.

"Let's just say you're a woman after my own tart."

"G-r-o-a-n," said Olympia, bending over and clutching her stomach.

It was all good fun, and Olympia was enjoying the lighthearted banter. Then she looked at the clock. Eileen Sullivan would be back in less than five minutes. She turned and started toward her office.

"The door's the other way," said Peggy McGrath, another one of the apron-wearing kitchen ladies. She was a tiny woman with twinkle in her eye that spoke volumes.

"I know, I just have to finish up something in my office. I'll check the lights and lock up when I leave."

"They gave you a key, then?"

"A key and a Salt Rock Parish Cookbook. What more do I need?"

"Not much. We're a good group, Reverend." Jocelyn was beaming with the pride of a long-time member and tireless worker. "Of course, we've got our characters. I saw you talking to Forrest Marsh. He's a piece of work, that one. We love him, but once he gets going he can talk your ears off."

Olympia remembered some of Frederick's more colorful descriptions of marathon talkers and carefully didn't share them. They were not exactly fitting and proper for conversation with a salt-of-the-earth Salt Rock church lady.

"Thanks for the advice, Jocelyn. I'll see you soon, I'm sure. I haven't decided when I'll be holding my regular office hours. I'll need to sort it out with the board and the church administrator before the end of the week. When I do, I'll put it in the newsletter. 'Bye for now."

"Oh, Reverend?"

Olympia turned back to Jocelyn. She was smiling proudly.

"I've got six recipes in that cookbook, one in each section."

"To quote my adorable English husband, I'm going to be fat as butter. Even so, I promise to look at them all."

Three

When Olympia returned to her office, she could see Eileen Sullivan, clutching her scarf to her chin, walking up the path. She set the plate of sweets on the bookcase next to the window and hurried to hold open the door so Eileen didn't have wait in the cold.

"Is it me, or is it even colder than it was this morning?"

"It's colder. The weather people said it was going to be a bad winter. It's supposed to be in the teens tonight; that's really cold for the Cape."

"I live on the other side of the canal. It's probably going to be even colder there, so I'm going to have to watch out for ice on side roads."

The two women were making meaningless small talk. Olympia knew Eileen would eventually get around to the reason for her being there, but now they were chatting, softening the edges of the space in the room and the distance between them. If she spoke too quickly, Eileen might bolt. Olympia had engaged in this kind of dance many times before. There was a distinct rhythm to it, advance and hold, advance and hold, and finally, the connection.

"Um, Reverend?"

"Yes, Eileen." Olympia spoke in soft voice.

The young woman sighed and looked down at her hands folded in her lap.

"Take another deep breath, and when you feel ready, try and tell me why you've come. I've already told you anything you say will be kept in confidence, but I can't be of any help until I know what's troubling you."

Eileen sat up a little straighter and poured it all out in one breath. "I'm Catholic, I'm pregnant, I'm afraid to tell my parents, I need to have an abortion, and I haven't a clue who to call or where to start looking. Everybody knows everybody down here–well, the year-rounders do anyway—so there's not one doctor I feel I can talk to."

"Doctors are like ministers. We are under oath to honor and keep a confidence."

Eileen shook her head. "Not here. My father's a doctor. They all know each other. Maybe there's someone in Boston, but like I said, I have no idea where to begin."

With this, her chin began to quiver, and tears rolled down her cheeks.

Olympia's heart was breaking, and at the same time, her mind was racing. At age seventeen she'd been in this very situation herself. At least Eileen was a bit older than that, and nowadays single motherhood was not the personal and familial disgrace it had been when it happened to her. Or was it? She reviewed the facts: Irish Catholic, traditional family, the father a doctor, and one terrified young woman, who had come in out of the cold, looking for help, sitting in front of her. She asked herself, how much of her own story should she disclose? Would it help? It was always a fine line, but Olympia had walked it before.

Why me? she silently asked herself. You know damn well why, came the answer, but only Olympia heard it. She stepped delicately out onto the thin ice that lay between them.

"Is abortion the only answer, Eileen?"

"It is as far as I'm concerned. You don't know my father. He's a really good man, and I'm the apple of his eye, his precious virgin daughter. I've always been his favorite. I just can't do this to him." More tears.

"But what about you? What would you do if you had a different set of parents, and they or religion weren't a factor in the decision or the outcome?"

Eileen made a face. "What are you talking about?"

"I'm trying to help you think about options. What do you know about Planned Parenthood?"

"Aren't they the people who give out condoms in high schools and leave them in public toilets?"

"They do a lot more than that. Certainly, they teach about contraception, but they also help women who are trying to get pregnant, and they help women who find themselves pregnant and don't want to be."

"Well, that's me, all right. Will they tell me where I can get an abortion? I'm twenty-one, so no one would have to sign for me."

Change direction, Olympia.

"How far along do you think you are?"

"About four weeks. I know exactly when it happened. I did an EPT test when I missed my period. It was positive." Eileen was sitting up straighter now and holding her hands against her stomach.

"I think as a first step you might go to Planned Parenthood. This is what they do, and they'll be able to talk you through all of your options."

"I only have one."

Okay, Olympia, say it.

"I'm not so sure. You see, I was in your situation many years ago, thirty-five, to be exact. Abortion was not an option. It wasn't legal anywhere, and the illegal ones were expensive and very dangerous. Lots of women died from botched abortions. It was bad enough being pregnant, but at least I knew enough not to risk my own life, as well."

Now Eileen Sullivan was all eyes and ears. She straightened up and leaned forward. "What happened? What did you do?"

"Like you, I was terrified of telling my parents, my mother especially. When I did, I was sent away to have the baby, and I had to put her up for adoption."

"Her? It was a girl?"

"It is a girl, and her name is Laura Wiltstrom. We've only recently reconnected."

Now it was Olympia's turn to get misty eyed, and she didn't bother to hide it.

"There's a chapter of Planned Parenthood in Providence, Rhode Island. Could I ask you to at least go down there and talk to them? Once you do, if you are still insistent on terminating the pregnancy, they'll give you the right advice and send you to a safe place to have it done."

"It sounds so final, terminating the pregnancy."

"It is very final, Eileen. That's why I'm asking you to think about it. I know enough about Roman Catholicism to know that abortion is a major sin, and I'm wondering where that is in your thinking."

Eileen made a face. "So is getting pregnant when you are not married, Reverend. The Catholic Church is very good about forgiving sins if you are truly repentant, and believe me, I am truly repentant. I'll never do this again."

"What are you saying?"

"I committed one big sin getting pregnant in the first place, and I'll commit another when I, uh, terminate the pregnancy. After that I'll go to confession in Boston, where nobody knows me, do my penance and come home. End of chapter."

"What about the man who's involved in this?" Olympia carefully didn't use the word father.

"He's nice. I really like him. We've been going out for almost a year. It's not like we planned it."

"Does he know?"

Eileen shook her head. "If I tell him, he might want to get married or something. I'm not ready for that, at least not now and under these circumstances. So I decided this will be my problem to solve, and then I'll see that happens after that."

It was not the time to bring up the idea that whoever the man was might have an interest in the outcome of this, but if the opportunity presented itself, she would.

"Young people in love, or even in like, are human, Eileen. Unplanned, um, events, can happen to the best of people in the most unexpected and unlikely circumstances. My paternal grandmother was Irish. She had fourteen pregnancies and raised nine children, and that was over eighty years ago. She always used to say, "First baby comes any time. After that, it takes nine months."

Eileen clapped her hand over her mouth and laughed out loud, and Olympia breathed the tiniest bit more easily.

"There's nothing new under the sun, my dear, and maybe most especially, unplanned pregnancies. Humans have hormones. God gave them to us, and under the right circumstances they seem to have minds of their own. Can I ask that you do one thing? Will you at least talk to the people at Planned Parenthood and then come back and see me before you do anything?"

"I don't have much time."

"I have the number right here. I can call them right now."

"I'd rather call them myself, if you don't mind."

This was either a good sign or a bad sign. Olympia didn't know which, and she wasn't going to push it. She didn't want to exert any pressure for fear the young woman might panic and bolt.

"They have a twenty-four-hour answering service. If you get a machine, at least you'll get their hours of operation, and you can call them back tomorrow. Do you have a car? Can you get there by yourself?"

Eileen nodded. "I'm supposed to be graduating from Salve Regina in June. My father gave me a car for an early graduation present. He said I would need it to get to interviews. Some interview, huh?"

Olympia waited before speaking. "Does that mean you will go and talk with them?"

"I'll talk with them."

Olympia dug around in her purse, fished out a pencil and scrap of paper and scribbled something down.

"Here are my church and home numbers. If you want to, you can call me after you've been to see them."

Eileen leaned back in her chair, folded her arms across her small bosom and looked directly at Olympia for the first time since she'd come in.

"I can't believe you are being so nice to someone you've never met. I guess I wasn't prepared for that."

"Remember, Eileen, I've been there. I know what this feels like. Even if I wasn't a minister when it happened, I'm still a woman and a mother, and there's no way I could just let you walk out of here without offering to help."

Eileen paused for a fraction of a second. "For the record, I didn't say I was actually going to go there. I'm only going to call them."

"I understand. If you do call them, they will let you know exactly what your options and your opportunities are, but they won't try to influence your final decision. I've worked with them before. They're kind and sympathetic. That's what you need right now, compassion and understanding, not somebody giving you hell because you are human and got carried away."

Eileen's eyebrows shot up. "Did I just hear you say hell?"

"You did indeed."

"I suppose I should be going." It was more of a question than a statement.

Olympia smiled and shook her head. "Only if you feel ready to. There's no rush. I don't have to be anywhere right away."

"No, I'm ready." She paused, "And I will call you." Then she stood and pulled on her coat. "I can't thank you enough. I don't … you …"

Olympia stood and held out her arms. "Let me give you a hug for the road and another one for good luck. If you lose my home number, you can always call the church and leave a number for me to call."

Olympia walked her outside, wished her Godspeed and then tugged the creaky old door shut against the biting wind. It was freezing out there. She stood by the window, watching and waiting until she saw Eileen's car turn left toward the lower Cape. Then, when she was well and truly gone, Olympia collected her own things and made ready to do the same. The plate of sweets left over from the coffee hour would provide a welcome diversion to what promised to be a thoughtful drive home, not that Olympia could do any more than she had already done. She hoped Eileen would, in fact, let her know of her final decision, but she knew in the end she might not.

This was another one of those curious aspects of her calling. Sometimes you had only one shot at helping someone. People you've never seen before can walk into your church or chapel, or you might walk into their hospital rooms. You sit with them for a time, listen to their stories, maybe say a prayer with them and never see or hear from them again.

Olympia tried to shake off the sense of responsibility she was already feeling for Eileen, but like a sticky-burr that she might pick up walking in the fall, it wouldn't be brushed off. What will be, will be, she tried telling herself, knowing full well she didn't believe a word of it.

Dutifully she walked around the church, checking the lights and the heat, and in so doing realized it would take her weeks to learn her way around the place. The building was over two hundred years old and had even more nooks and crannies than her antique home in Brookfield. Over time some rooms had been changed and expanded, and others had been completely walled off as the congregation grew, and their needs changed. Old buildings like this had secret lives of their own.

As she pulled the door shut behind her and rattled the doorknob to make sure it was firmly locked, she wondered what she might find in some of those long-forgotten secret corners. A good project for an idle afternoon, she told herself as she turned into the bitter wind and sprinted toward her van.

Four

When Olympia arrived home she found Frederick with his pale blue eyes tightly closed, his bewhiskered chin resting on his chest, spark out in front of the fire. The two cats, Cadeau and Thunderfoot, were similarly unconscious and tangled over his crossed legs. Cadeau, the sleek black one, raised his head, flicked an ear and opened one green eye in greeting but didn't bother getting up. So much for unconditional love, Olympia thought before backing out of the sitting room and tiptoeing into the kitchen in search of food and drink.

It didn't take long to make herself a pot of hot chocolate—sugar free, of course, assemble a grilled cheese and tomato sandwich with a light smear of Dijon mustard, and snag a couple of cookies off the church plate. With all of this arranged on a tea tray, she slipped into her own chair on the other side of the fire, eased off her shoes and settled in for some seriously mindless relaxing. Frederick opened one eye and pointed it in her direction.

"I say, that smells heavenly. Did you leave any *chocolat pour moi*?" Frederick often sprinkled French words into conversation. "For your poor thirsty and be-catted Englishman?"

Much as she loved him, at that precise moment Olympia could have throttled him. By mutual agreement, if one or the other had a cat or two in his lap, that person was excused from doing anything until said feline chose to vacate the premises.

"I made a whole pot." She set her tray down on the footstool next to her chair. "It's still hot. I'll be right back.

You want some cookies, I mean, biscuits? The ladies at church sent some home with me."

"Oooh, you do know how to treat a man, don't you?" He was beaming at her.

"Let's just say I've had months of practice. How long have we been married now?"

"Five months, three weeks and four days, but who's counting?"

Olympia yelled from the kitchen. "Are you serious? Have you really kept count?

"Lucky guess, my darling. How did this morning go? What are they like?"

"Interesting," said Olympia, holding out a mug and a plate to Frederick.

"Uh oh. That's one of those innocent words you use when you don't want to commit yourself. Out with it, darling. What did you find? A dead body in the front pew? The skeleton of a vicar from the Mayflower in the coat closet? Somebody's poisoned the communion wine?"

"We don't use communion wine," she snorted.

"Don't change the subject, and don't keep me waiting. What's our next clerical cliffhanger going to be?"

He was answered by a familiar ping from the antique clock on the mantle over the woodstove that sounded only when their resident house-ghost, Miss Winslow, wanted their attention.

"Frederick! Don't make fun of me. It's not as if I go looking for trouble."

Olympia glanced up at the clock and shrugged. Another ping. She glared up at the clock.

"And you keep out of this."

"I'm not convinced of that," he mumbled.

"What did you just say?"

Frederick gazed up at the ceiling. "Mmm, lovely biscuits, these, so we know you won't starve. Now tell me all about these good people."

"This was my first Sunday. I haven't even met all of them yet."

"Olympia, when you start dodging the subject, it usually means you're well on the way to getting involved or even embroiled in something that is less than savory. By now I'm used to it. Why don't you give me your impression of the congregation as a whole and then tell me about the ones you met today?"

"As a group they seem pretty healthy. The church building is old, but it's well kept. They know their jobs, and they do them. There seems to be a good feeling among them, lots of friendly chatter and gentle joking. There's an older gentleman who is a bit of a character, but everybody seems to love him."

"I'm waiting. I know there's more. Which one's the axe murderer?"

"Oh, for God's sake, Frederick."

"Olympia?"

"Well, if you must know I did have a young woman come in out of the cold, looking for help. She's not a member, and she's not an axe murderer. She's Catholic and pregnant, and she walked in right after the service, hoping she could find someone to talk to."

"And you invited her to come and live with us."

Olympia rolled her eyes. "No, I didn't. I sat with her, listened to her story and gave her my telephone number and the contact information for Planned Parenthood. Then I gave her an encouraging hug and sent her on her way."

"That's all?" Frederick gave her an incredulous look.

"So far, anyway. She may or may not come back. She didn't give me her contact information, so I don't think she will. Hell, I'm not even sure if she gave me her right name. She might not have, you know. She's in a real panic over this. Planned Parenthood is the right place for her."

"It's not like you to let her go without some kind of follow up."

"What else could I do? I can't force myself on her. She knows where to find me, I made sure of that, poor kid." Olympia shook her head, remembering the fear and desperation in the girl's eyes.

"Is that all? No axe murderers?"

"Well …" Olympia made a face.

"I knew it."

"More of a pest than a problem, really."

"Explain."

"It's a woman in her early forties with a classic case of insecure approval-seeking combined with compulsive people-pleasing behavior. I've encountered it before. They usually latch on to an authority figure and do everything possible to make that person like them. Seems like I've got one of those on my hands."

"How do you deal with that?" Frederick was managing to stroke both cats with one hand and not spill his cocoa with the other. Olympia was impressed.

"Lots of honest affirmation, along with the establishment of clear personal and professional boundaries. That usually takes care of it."

"And if it doesn't?"

"They typically have two reactions. One is to up the ante. They start doing more and more to get the target's attention until it works."

"And the other is?"

"They can get nasty. You know, the vengeful spurned lover kind of reaction. I don't know where this one is on the spectrum, but I'll know day after tomorrow when I have a meeting with her."

He looked puzzled. "So soon? You just started."

"I've found if you can assure someone like this early on that you like her just the way she is, and she doesn't have to do anything more to earn your approval, she will usually calm down."

"What if she doesn't?"

"Then we have another meeting. Relax, darling, it's not the first time I've encountered this. Every so often, when I was at the college, a student would develop a crush or a hero worship thing for me. It happens, and I've learned from experience that kind words really do turn away wrath—or in this case, will most likely mollify Emily Goodale. Either way, it's nothing I want to spend any more time on right now. What will be, will be. I'm only there for three months, remember? Then I'm out. I don't have to change the world down there, I just have to hold it together."

Frederick looked doubtful but brightened immediately when his lady love changed the subject to something more tangible.

"Now as I remember, we were going to talk about turning the store room off the kitchen into an office for yours truly. Have you given that any further thought while I was out?"

"I have indeed. Let me divest myself of these two cats, and I'll show you what I've got up to."

Now it was Olympia's turn to look doubtful. "You, uh, got up to? Don't tell me you've already started. I thought we were going to discuss it first." Her doubtfulness was now bordering on frantic panic, but she was doing her best not to let it show. She didn't like to squelch his enthusiasm.

"Now I know you mentioned expanding the space and knocking out a wall."

He was talking over his shoulder now, leading her into the back entryway, which led to the aforementioned space.

Olympia winced, took a deep cleansing breath and followed the man she loved.

Behind the Salt Rock Village meeting house, Emily Goodale parked her car and let herself in through the private door to the minister's study. She'd neglected to take the altar flowers with her that morning and wanted to retrieve them before somebody threw them out. Usually the church ladies took the Sunday flowers to elderly members of the congregation, along with a copy of the church bulletin and a few little treats from the coffee hour, but Emily had a different plan. She liked to put flowers on the graves in the church yard. Most were so old the names and dates were worn away, and no one tended them other than to mow the grass and pull the weeds; but they were part of church history, and Emily liked to spend time with them.

She felt sorry for these long forgotten forefathers and mothers of her precious church. And so, when it was her turn to do the Sunday flowers, she honored their individual and collective memories by placing a single flower at the base of each headstone. There were exactly twenty-seven. She'd counted them any number of times just to make sure. Because she didn't want anyone to be left out, she always brought a couple of extra flowers just to make sure.

The air temperature was dropping faster now, and Emily made quick work of her solitary ritual. When she finished, she slipped back into the minister's study and left one remaining flower on Olympia's desk. The other she slipped inside her coat to keep it warm.

Eileen Sullivan was parked in the middle of a supermarket parking lot in East Orleans. She was holding her cell phone to her ear and making notes on the back of a pew card she'd picked up in Olympia's church earlier in the day.

As luck would have it, Frederick had not removed the back wall of the storage room. He had only moved some of the accumulated detritus which had been piled and tossed and totally forgotten in there for who knew how many years. Now they could at least see across the room to the back wall, even if they couldn't yet get to it. They really hadn't done anything with that room since they started living there other than look into it, then turn away and slam the door. There always seemed to be something else that was more important. But now Frederick would have something to do on the days when he wasn't working in the bookstore, and it was too cold to be out in the garden. At least that was the plan. To be continued, thought Olympia, and suggested they call out for a pizza.

Five

After breakfast the next morning, wearing woolly hats and their winter coats, Frederick and Olympia revisited the back room. From the doorway they could see pieces of broken and discarded furniture, an antique steamer trunk, a box of old bottles, piles of rags or clothing and evidence of more than one colony of little animals likely still in residence. Olympia wrinkled her nose. At her feet, Cadeau eagerly twitched his. There was a distinct mousey smell to the place, and the cat, ears forward, was vibrating.

What light there was came from a single grimy window on the back wall. The remains of what might have been a flowered chintz curtain, now faded and tattered, hung off a rusted hook on the top left corner of the window frame.

"We're going to need either a bulldozer or a front end loader to get through all this junk," said Olympia.

"We don't want to rush, my love. Who knows what we might find in all of this. Remember, this place goes back to the 1700s. There might be some real treasures hidden here.

"More like vintage mouse turds," said Olympia, wrinkling her nose and turning away. "Whew, this place needs a fumigator, as well."

"Oh, you are romantic," laughed Frederik. "I'm looking forward to picking through this. It will give me something to do on these cold, dark days while you're off saving souls at that little church of yours."

"You'll need to dress warmly when you do; it's freezing out here."

"So I suppose we'll have to think about heating, as well," said Frederick.

"Don't get ahead of yourself, darling. One thing at a time."

"But …"

"No buts. This afternoon when I get home, we're going back out there and take measurements. Then we'll sit down with a piece of graph paper and sketch out the possibilities. If you absolutely must get started on something, then see if you can wrestle that trunk free. When I get back we'll look and see if there's anything inside that's worth keeping or selling."

Frederic was mollified and nodded in enthusiastic agreement. "Jolly good! It has to be at least two hundred years old, and it might well be worth a bob or two on its own.

"Think of it as hunting without a gun. It's treasure for the taking."

"And it's all ours. Why …"

'And it all stinks," said Olympia, interrupting him. "The first thing you should do is get that window open and let in some fresh air. I don't care if it is the dead of winter. This place has never been heated, so everything in here is used to being frozen stiff."

"What time did you say you were leaving?" Frederick was smiling his most ingratiating smile. Olympia recognized it and felt a slight frisson of anxiety, which she wisely kept to herself. That particular grin of his could mean anything; she'd seen it before. She would trust God and hope for the best. She smiled back.

"Right after I have another cup of coffee, husband dearest. Shall I pour one for you?"

Olympia planned to arrive at the church shortly after eleven. Today she would sit with Charlotte, the church administrator, and Catherine Allen, the president of the board, to sort out her office hours and list what, if anything, they would like her to do while she was in residence. The original agreement had been relatively clear: cover the duties of the regular minister, hold the place together, ask for help if necessary, and don't make waves.

Then there were the unspoken traditions and sacred cows. Every organization had them, ways of doing things and people who did them that were never in the bylaws but were understood and observed by all. Woe betide the person who ignored them. These were what Olympia wanted to learn about and respect. Such inside information could make or break even a short ministry. That much she did know, and she hadn't learned it in seminary, although she dearly wished they would find a way to teach it. This was on the job training, learned through experience, observation and, ultimately, paying attention.

These thoughts and more were chasing each other around inside her head along with images of irascible old Forrest Marsh and his twinkling eyes, Emily Goodale and her hungry eyes, and Eileen Sullivan and her desperate eyes.

"It's only day two, and I've already got myself a full plate," she told the rear view mirror as she wheeled her vintage VW van into the church parking lot. She looked up at the towering white steeple, stark against the electric blue sky. "Here I am, God, ready to go. Good morning, church, and just what holy mysteries do you have in store for me today?"

When she got inside, Charlotte, Catherine and a fresh pot of coffee were awaiting her in the Ladies Parlor. Olympia greeted the two of them and accepted the cup of coffee that was held out to her.

"Sit wherever you want," said Catherine. "They're all uncomfortable, but this room is the pride and joy of the Women's Alliance. I'm sure some of the chairs came over on the Mayflower—at least they feel like it. And do stay away from the Victorian sofa. It's got a horsehair seat, and I swear it bites."

Olympia laughed, took a grateful sip of the steaming coffee, chose a carved oak rocking chair and then addressed them both.

"Thank you so much for agreeing to come in today. I think when you are new in a place it really helps to have a sit-down with people who have been there for a while. You two know the history of this church and all the major players. If there's anything you think I should or must know, please don't ever hesitate to tell me, and don't wait for a staff meeting either. Okay?"

To their confused faces she added, "I mean, if there's someone who's in the hospital or needs a home visit, or if someone is having troubles at home. I don't mean gossip, mind you, but I can't minister to people if I don't know what they need. I need more eyes and ears than the ones God gave me. I hope I can depend on you two."

Catherine brightened. "Now I understand. Of course. Reverend Phil, he's our regular minister; he's been here for years. He's a good man and works way too hard. We're all really happy that he's taking a little time for himself. He needs it."

Olympia smiled and nodded in agreement.

"I don't know him personally, but I know he's very well thought of. I also know that it's hard to let go of someone you love and trust and invite a relative stranger to do his job for three months, no matter how highly they were recommended. I'm used to that. That's why I'm talking to you now. I'm not trying to fill his shoes. I'm only trying to keep things in order until he comes back. There's a real difference between the two. So I need to know anything that either of you thinks might need attending to, if not right now, then over the next three months."

"I understand," said Catherine. "It's just that there are a self-selected few here who do most of the work and are always complaining about how overworked they are."

"On the other side of the coin, there's always another one or two who always seem to be on the outside looking in and complaining about that," added Charlotte.

Olympia chuckled. "Nothing new under the sun, is there? Well, don't expect miracles. I didn't take that course in seminary, but knowing who is where on the spectrum will certainly help. I really want to do my best for all of you while I'm here."

"I believe you do," said Catherine, "and I'm glad you're here. It will be a nice change to have a woman in the pulpit— you know, a fresh perspective. Reverend Phil is good, but men see things one way, and women often see them differently."

"And *vive la différence*," said Olympia.

"With that bit of wisdom, I think I should get back to my desk," said Charlotte. You two sort out the details and let me know when you'll be having your office hours, Olympia. That way I can post them in the church newsletter. Shall I shut the door?"

Catherine nodded and changed the subject. "I saw you talking to Forrest yesterday. Isn't he a hoot? He's deaf as a post and smart as a whip, that one. What his ears don't hear, his eyes never miss. He's adored by one and all. It's a true blessing he's so fit for his age. I can't think what this place would be like without him."

"By the look of him, I think he'll be around for a good while yet. And yes, he's an old charmer."

"Don't think he doesn't know it," said Catherine with a fond smile.

"Anything else I should be aware of that you feel comfortable saying? As I said, this really isn't a gossip session, and I hope it doesn't sound that way. My mother always used to say that forewarned is forearmed."

Catherine nodded. "Then I should probably tell you about Jeremy Adams."

"Was he here on Sunday?"

"Probably. He usually is."

Olympia looked puzzled. "I don't understand."

Catherine settled into to the story. "He was one of the founding fathers of this church. His family donated the money to have the original meeting house built. Of course, we've added to it over the years, but the sanctuary dates back to the late 1700s. Most of the boxed pews are from that period. Many still have the family nameplates nailed on the doors. In the 1800s his grandson donated the money for the church organ. It's an original Hook, and it was made right here in New England."

Olympia looked more confused than ever, and Catherine was enjoying the game.

"But if he was one of the original members, how could he be here? Oh, wait a minute. I think I'm beginning to understand. Are you telling me you have a ghost here?"

"We prefer to think of him as a spirited benefactor, but yes, we most definitely have a ghost here. We don't often see him, but we can sense his presence, particularly in the organ loft. Does that bother you?"

Olympia laughed. "Not in the least. I might even introduce him to my Miss Winslow. Is he married?"

Now it was Catherine's turn to look confused. In a conspiratorial whisper, Olympia shared the history and histrionics of her own beloved Leanna Faith Winslow.

When she finished, both women were smiling and talking about going out to lunch to continue the visit. Catherine was an engaging and no nonsense person. She would also be a valuable ally in the weeks and months to come, thought Olympia, and in this business you never know when you'll need one.

She started to get up, but Catherine waved her back down. "Before we go, there is one more thing I should mention. I saw you talking with Emily Goodale yesterday. I'm sure you figured out that she's got some problems."

Olympia was wise enough not to agree but said only, "She does seem quite anxious to be of help."

Catherine frowned and pursed her lips, choosing her words carefully. "More than a little, and I don't want to speak badly of her. I'm just telling you what I've observed. She's relatively new here. I think she's been with us less than a year, but she's been in and out of most of the churches up and down the Cape. She says she suffers from depression, but that could be her own diagnosis. Either way, she seems to grab onto someone and becomes the instant new best friend. Then, just as quickly, something happens, and she's looking around for someone new to latch onto. She's not a bad person, more like … What is it the young folks say now? She's high maintenance."

"Hmm," said Olympia.

"I wouldn't have said anything, except you asked, and seeing her following you around on Sunday makes me think you might be next in line. I should also tell you, she didn't get on well with Phil Rutledge."

Olympia elected not to say that she already knew that. "I appreciate your telling me this. It's useful information, Catherine. Now where are we going for that lunch? We can talk more when I have hot food in front of me, and my stomach isn't growling. What time is it? I left my watch at home."

"It's almost quarter to one. No wonder you're hungry."

Six

In Brookfield, Frederick put down his book, eased Cadeau off his lap and made ready to start his day. It was noon. He dutifully donned a warm jacket and woolly hat, and stuck a mismatched pair of gloves in his pocket before heading into battle. He could hear the cats wailing from inside the kitchen, but he didn't want to risk their health and safety by letting them run loose in the chaos he was about to create. Frederick liked a bit of chaos now and then. He called it working clutter. It made him happy to be surrounded, literally, by the falling and flying shrapnel of his latest project. Olympia truly didn't understand this side of him, and maybe she never would, but here, alone with his thoughts and a sledge hammer, Frederick was his own man.

Yesterday evening Olympia had suggested that he might begin by going through the trunk, but when she got home she was too tired, and they'd agreed to wait. Today was going to be window day. Olympia had said that a wall should be opened up to let in more light, and there was no time like the present to make it happen.

"Let battle commence," said Frederick to no one in particular, and with the door to the kitchen tightly closed behind him, he advanced on the hapless back wall with a gleam in his eye he usually reserved for private moments with his lady love.

When they returned from lunch, Catherine wished Olympia a pleasant afternoon and dropped her off in the church parking lot. Once inside the building, she discovered that Charlotte had gone for the day but had left a note taped to the door.

Hi, sorry I missed you. If you have time, e-mail me your office hours, and I'll post them. One phone call: Emily Goodale confirming 11 a.m. tomorrow. I'll need your sermon title and hymns by Wednesday. I'm in on Mon., Wed., Thurs., 9-12. See you soon. C.

Alone in the silent church, Olympia decided to go exploring. She respected and admired old buildings—so much so, she'd bought one herself. She loved to walk around, listening to the echo of her own footsteps, and imagine all the things that had happened within these walls over the centuries. Churches are second homes to many folk. She knew that. As she moved from room to room she thought about the couples who began their married lives here, the babies that were christened here, and the funeral and memorial services where people said goodbye for the last time. She promised herself she'd ask for the church records and see for herself what names and connections she might find. It was, after all, a building almost as old as her own home. Why, I might even find a connection to Miss Winslow, she thought. It was certainly not out of the realm of possibility.

Thus mentally occupied, she methodically made her way from room to room. She was trying to determine which parts were original, which were relatively new, and what the progression from then to now might have been. The building was cold, and she was beginning to shiver. The thermostat was set to fifty-five degrees, but in the unlit emptiness of the echoing old place, it seemed much colder. She made her way around the parish hall, then out into the entryway, which led to the sanctuary, and was on her way back to start downstairs when she heard the phone in her office ringing. She reversed direction and sprinted toward her office, managing to grab it just as the message came on.

"Hello, Salt Rock Fellowship, this is Reverend Olympia Brown speaking."

"Oh! I didn't expect you to be there. This is Eileen Sullivan. I just wanted to thank you for being so kind to me yesterday and to let you know that I'm parked outside the Planned Parenthood building. I thought about what you said, and then I read about them on line, and it all checked out just as you told me. They'll help me do what I need to do, and I won't be risking my life, and my parents will never find out. So I guess I just called to thank you."

Olympia thought fast. "I'm glad you called, Eileen, and if you want to come up and talk with me again, I have the time."

"Oh, thank you, but I don't want to bother you more than I already have."

"I'm a minister, Eileen, it's no bother. I'm usually in the office Monday, Wednesday and Thursday mornings. You still have my home number, don't you?"

"I do, Reverend, thank you. Maybe I'll call you again when it's over. I might need to talk to someone then."

Olympia was clenching and unclenching her fists in total frustration. This was so delicate. She couldn't push, nor could she appear to be disinterested. Find the balance, Olympia.

"I'm here if you need me, but I'll say it again. It might be good to talk to someone before you take any … definitive action."

"I don't have much time, Reverend I just want this over."

And the wrong decision could scar you for a lifetime, thought Olympia.

"Hear them out, Eileen, and then make your decision. Meanwhile, I'll pray for you."

"Thank you, Reverend. You've been very kind."

It was only when she turned to hang up the phone that she noticed the white carnation, limp and wilting, lying on her desk. Thinking she might still be able to revive it, she carried it out to the kitchen, cut off over half the stem and stuck it in a vase she found in one of the cabinets. Carnations were determined little things, and so, it appeared, was Emily Goodale. Olympia was in no doubt who had left it there. The only question in her mind was, when had she done it?

With the carnation on life support and sitting on the corner of her desk, Olympia decided to put off her explorations of the lower level of the church for another day and go home. She wanted to be sure to be on the road before it even started to get dark. That way she could enjoy the scenic drive through the sweet little towns and villages which were the very hallmark of Cape Cod.

She'd always enjoyed driving. She found it was a time to think and ponder and sort out problems without interruption. Just as often as not, she didn't even turn on the radio but preferred to drive in silence, letting her mind wander wherever it might. It could, however, be disturbing to be turning into her driveway with no memory of how she got there until she realized that, too, was part of her thinking process. Jim called it driving on autopilot. She preferred to think of it as The Zone, and she was perfectly content to be there. For the time being there was nothing more she could do for Eileen Sullivan, and Emily Goodale was on hold until tomorrow. She added sermon title to the tomorrow list and realized she was already crossing the Sagamore Bridge.

As she turned onto her street, Olympia remembered she and Frederick were going to sketch out a plan for how to proceed with the conversion of the store room. That'll be fun, she thought. He does enjoy a good project, and I've not had my own space since he moved in. Much as I love him, I definitely need a room of my own.

Once in and divested of her winter layers, she found Frederick in the sitting room with both cats in rapt attention, digging through the contents of one of the boxes he'd dragged in from the storage room.

"Find anything interesting yet?"

"Depends on how you define interesting. There are some old books and magazines, mostly from the 1940s and '50s. It's likely a lot of this stuff came from previous owners and tenants. There's nothing old enough to qualify as a real antique. I believe your word is vintage. On the other hand, vintage is becoming quite fashionable these days, is it not?"

"Depends on how you define vintage," she retorted, "but I agree, none of it looks or smells very exciting."

"We'll never know until we check out every last bit."

"Agreed, my dear, but how about a glass of wine to make the task a bit more fun?"

He gave her a very American thumbs up and followed with a very British, "Jolly good."

When she returned, glasses in hand and a bag of Doritos under her arm, Frederick was setting the last of the contents of the box on the carpet beside her chair. None of it was heart stopping: a pair of dried out leather shoes, a moth-eaten sweater, another book and some old sheet music.

"I think we can consign most of this to the dustbin, Olympia. Do you see anything you want?"

"As far as I'm concerned, you can chuck it all. Did you make any kind of construction progress out there?"

"A bit," said Frederick. He was carefully examining the palm of his hand.

"Don't you remember? We were going to take measurements and come up with a plan."

"Mmm," said Frederick, turning his attention to the back of his hand.

"Frederick, is something the matter? Come on, go find your tape measure, and let's go out there."

"Before we do, I think I should let you know that I sort of already got started, but then I changed my mind and thought it might be better to do as you suggested and start with the boxes."

Technicolor memories of spilled paint and a boarded-up kitchen door flashed through her mind, and they weren't pretty.

"Frederick, what exactly did you do out there?"

"Well, let's just say you've got some nice fresh air out there now. You did say you wanted that, didn't you?"

Seven

With no small flutterings of anxiety, Olympia followed Frederick out to the scene of the crime and stood back as he opened the door. They were hit with a blast of fresh cold air—very fresh cold air—blowing straight at them through a jagged hole in the back wall.

Olympia knew better than to shriek. Instead, she waited as Frederick selected his words. He cleared his throat.

"You said to open the window. So after I cracked the frame and broke the glass, I figured there was no point in stopping and might as well finish the job, so I did. Much more efficient that way, don't you think, considering we'd most likely be replacing the whole thing anyway?"

"Well, we certainly will be now," she said through chattering teeth.

"You're not upset, are you?"

"No, Frederick, I'm too damn cold to be mad. Shut the door, and let's go back where it's warm and think about what we might need to do next."

"Uh, would you like another glass of wine?"

Right now I could use bottle of wine, thought Olympia. "Just a half, or I won't be able to make our supper." She smiled sweetly.

After supper the two did work out a plan for the doom-room, as Olympia was now calling it. Step one was to nail a tarp over the window to keep out any rain or snow, and after that string an overhead light so that, without any sort of natural light source, they could see what they were doing.

"I did measure it," said Frederick. "It's about ten feet by twelve feet, give or take a few inches. Of course, considering its probable age, there's probably not a level spot or square corner in the place."

They were interrupted from any further discussion by the sound of Olympia's cell phone squawking frantically from somewhere in her handbag. She caught it in time to hear Eileen Sullivan leaving a message. Olympia bit her lip and waited until the girl finished before she spoke.

"Eileen, its Olympia. I heard the message, are you okay?"

"Not really," came the reply. "Can I take you up on that offer to talk with you again before I, uh, do anything?"

Oh, thank God. Olympia willed her voice to be steady. "Of course. I'll be in my office at the church all day tomorrow. Will that work?"

"Sure, what time?"

"Can you wait until after lunch, say, one o'clock?" Olympia didn't want any crossover between Eileen and the dear, dependent Emily.

"I'll be there. Thank you, Reverend."

Olympia hung up the phone and blew out a long breath.

"That didn't sound good," said Frederick.

"I don't think it was. I'll know tomorrow. That was my little Irish Catholic pregnant waif. She did go and talk to the people at Planned Parenthood, that's the good news, but it sounds as if she's decided to terminate the pregnancy."

"Well, that will certainly solve the problem, won't it?"

"Yes and no. That's probably what she wants to talk about."

"I don't understand."

"She's stumbling through a theological and emotional minefield. For many people, and not just Catholics, abortion is the most heinous of sins. It's no less than murder. If she goes ahead with it, she's willfully committing a perilous sin. If she doesn't, she risks a lifetime of shame, the alienation of her family, and she'll begin her adult life as a single mother."

Frederick rubbed his chin. "I'm not being dismissive when I say I'm glad all I have to do is knock out the occasional window. That, at least, can be replaced. This poor woman doesn't seem to have that option."

"Right in one, Frederick. No one can make that decision for her, and whichever way it goes, the process will be agonizing, and the outcome is at best uncertain."

"She's not even a member of your church."

"It's not my church, Frederick. We don't own these churches, we serve them; but it is my problem to deal with because she came to me, and I chose to respond. If she were a member of the congregation, I'd call the regular minister at once, but the purpose of a sabbatical is to go off and partake of spiritual and physical refreshment. I want to be able to give that to him. I can handle this."

"If anyone can, you can, my dear, but I don't envy you this one."

"There is no perfect solution. I'll just do the best I can and trust that divine grace will guide both of us."

"Oh, yes, and speaking of divine grace, Jim called while you were out. He says he's got some news, but he wants to share it over a stellar bottle of wine. I told him you'd call him and arrange a time."

Olympia smiled fondly at the thought of her best friend. He did like to build suspense, that one. But what the hell, he'd been through enough to allow himself this small indulgence. She wondered what it might be. With the changes Jim had undergone in the last two years, she wouldn't be surprised at much of anything. Most of all she wanted him to find fulfillment in his life and work, and then maybe someone to love, or was that asking too much?

"Earth to Olympia," said Frederick. "Are you in that tantalizing body sitting across from me, or is it merely wishful thinking? Your mind is certainly out in the stratosphere."

"I'm here. I was just thinking about Jim. I'll go give him a call. We're not doing anything this week, are we?"

"I don't know about the rest of the week, but I have a very definite plan for the rest of the evening. It may or may not result in extraterrestrial travel, but I do suspect if we proceed without caution, we might feel the earth move."

Olympia laughed out loud. "Why, you delightful old lecher. Let me call Jim and barricade the cats in the kitchen, and I'll see you anon."

She switched her phone back on and started to dial Jim's number while an extraordinarily cheery Frederick bounced out to the kitchen to attend to the cats.

"Hi, Jim, It's Olympia, Frederick just told me you want to bring us glad tidings of great joy along with a bottle of superb wine—red or white?"

"A semi-dry white from Oregon, and I do indeed have some good news. How about dinner sometime this week?"

"Well, then, how about tomorrow? I just started a sabbatical fill-in at a church on the Cape, so I've got regular hours, but I'm the one who makes them. Also, now that I think about it, I could use your advice and wisdom on something I'm dealing with here."

"Oh, dear God, Olympia …"

"Don't even start down that path, Jim. It has nothing to do with the church which, by the way, is really quite sweet. "

"In other words, so far, so good on the pastoral front," said Jim.

"No problems there, Jim. No, this involves a woman, specifically not a member of the church, who literally came in out of the cold looking for help. She's a devout Catholic, pregnant, and says she wants an abortion."

"Ouch. What did you say to her?"

"I did nothing other than to listen. I did get her to go to Planned Parenthood, and now that she has, she's asked to talk with me again tomorrow."

"What are you going to say?"

"I'm going to do what I did before. I'm going to listen and help her sort out her options. Frankly, even though I'm pro-choice, I don't think abortion would be the best option for her."

"Are you going to tell her that?"

"I've just had an idea. If she's willing, would you come down and talk to her? You are still a priest, and you were Roman Catholic, so you'd understand this better than anyone."

Olympia looked up to see a stark naked Frederick leering at her from their bedroom doorway.

"Uh, Jim, something's just come up. Can I call you tomorrow after I've talked to her?"

Later, after the earth had indeed moved for both of them and Frederick was deeply asleep, Olympia quietly slipped out of the marital bed and went into the sitting room. Now, sitting by the woodstove with a cup of tea, she was trying to sort through the troublesome thoughts that were keeping her awake. Finally, she put down her cup and reached for Miss Winslow's diary. Over the years she'd been living there, she'd learned that when something was troubling her, she often found guidance in the words of a woman who'd lived over a hundred fifty years ago, a woman not unlike herself, who lived and loved and struggled with her own curious turns of fortune within and beyond these very walls.

February 2, 1863

Only Richard and Louisa know of this, but I have completed my first novel, Bright Days, Dark Nights, *and sent it off to a publisher recommended to me by the editor of Godey's. I shall know soon if it is to be published, but with the cold and the heavy snows we have had to endure this year, who knows when the mail will next be delivered? My greater concern is for Aunt Louisa. She is taken with a most terrible cold and has remained abed these last three days. It is most unlike her. Still, she does not complain and puts on far too brave a face when we ask how she is faring. The hardest thing for her is that little Jonathan may not visit for fear he might fall ill as well. He's too young to understand.*

I do wish she would eat more. Richard made a fine broth of chicken and vegetables, but after a few sips, she smiled and turned away and soon drifted back to sleep.

I cannot allow myself even to think the worst. If only this awful cold would let up, and we could bring her outside for some fresh air. I'm certain that would brighten her eyes and put some color back into her cheeks. Meanwhile I watch and wait, and when time permits, I write.

More anon, LFW

Eight

Olympia was feeling somewhat ragged when she unlocked the church door on Tuesday morning. It was well after midnight when she fell asleep, and even though she managed to catch an extra hour in the morning, she still felt wobbly around the edges.

The church was chilly and empty. She remembered too late that this was not one of Charlotte's days and resolved to hold her office hours from then on when the woman was in the outer office. Not that Olympia had any particular fears; Cape Cod was hardly a high-crime area. It just made sense not to be alone for hours at a time in a semi-public empty building where anyone might walk in.

Luckily she had a thermostat in her office so she didn't have to heat the whole building to keep warm while she worked. After turning up the heat, Olympia wrapped her coat around her shoulders and listened to the clicking and ticking in the radiator as the heat come up. It was 10:45 a.m. Emily would be there shortly. She thought about making a pot of tea, but when she heard the sound of the main door opening and approaching footsteps, she put it on hold for the moment. The ritual of making and sipping tea was a good icebreaker and an anxiety diffuser. She'd used it many times in the past, and it usually worked.

"Reverend?"

Olympia stood up and extended a hand over her desk in greeting. "Hi, Emily, come in and sit down. You might want to leave your coat on. It's freezing in here. I forgot that

Charlotte doesn't come in today. I just turned up the heat. If you're cold, we can go out in the kitchen and make some tea."

"No, that's okay, I had a coffee on the way over." Emily looked around the room and then glanced at the door she'd just come through. "So it's just us?"

"Just us and the church mice."

"I don't suppose you know about Jeremy Adams. Have they told you about him?"

Olympia smiled and nodded. "I just started here last week, remember. Maybe he's waiting to be formally introduced."

Emily responded with an uncomprehending stare, and Olympia decided to get down to the business at hand.

"So, help me get to know you. Did you grow up around here?" Olympia learned long ago that a really safe place to start a conversation with someone she didn't know was to ask about the town or city where they grew up. Local geography was usually safe and nonthreatening.

"I grew up in hell, Reverend," said Emily, "and that's what I need to talk about."

Olympia gulped. Not much shocked her these days, but she'd been totally caught off guard with the venom and the vehemence with which the mousey-looking woman spat out the words. As an attention getter, it had the desired effect, and it was exactly what Emily had intended to do.

Olympia decided to toss the ball straight back at her. "Well, that certainly leaves no room for imagination, but it does beg for clarification. Why don't you tell me what you'd like me to know about that?"

"About what?"

Olympia had deliberately left the response open ended. "You just said you grew up in hell. That might be a good place to start. Why don't you tell me more about that?"

Now Emily was the one caught off guard. She stammered and moved into more familiar waters. "Maybe I'll start with what happened when I first started coming here. I moved to the Cape about six months ago. I didn't know anyone, and joining a church is a good way to meet people you can trust. I mean, they wouldn't be going to a church if they weren't nice, right?"

Olympia nodded. "I'm new here, too, remember. I'm still getting to know people, and if first impressions are worth anything at all, this is a lovely place, don't you think? I'm delighted to be here even if it is only for three months."

Emily chewed on a corner of her lip and continued. "I'm still deciding. When I first came here, it seemed friendly enough, but now it seems that everybody has their own little things, and it's hard to find where I might fit in."

"I think being new to anything is a bit difficult. It always takes me a while to scope something out and find out who does what before I'm comfortable in a new situation."

Emily sat up straighter. "Really? You, too?"

"Yup, me, too, and because of the type of ministry I have, I'm often in new situations, so I know how unsettled you can feel. You've heard of substitute teachers; well, I'm sort of a substitute minister. When a regular minister has to be away for a period of time, I sign a contract to fill in for that period."

"You do this for a living. I was in a lot of new situations, too. That's kind of what I meant when I said I grew up in hell. I was in foster care until I was eighteen, and if you can survive that, you can survive anything. You know what I mean?"

Olympia knew a loaded question when she heard one, and she wasn't buying into it.

"Actually, I don't. The foster parents I've met have been wonderful, dedicated people who want to help give kids a break. I know there are some bad ones, because I read about them in the newspapers. However, like you said earlier, the ones who bring their kids to church are people who want to instill good values in the children in their care."

"I wasn't so lucky."

"Is that what you want to tell me about?"

Emily nodded and went on to tell Olympia how, as a child, she'd been shuffled from one appalling situation to the next. In her troubled journey she'd suffered physical and sexual abuse, infrequent to nonexistent medical and dental care, and an interrupted education. On her own at eighteen, she'd trained to be a Certified Nursing Assistant, known commonly as a CNA. Since then, she'd always been able to find work because she didn't mind cleaning up people's puke and shit.

Olympia shuddered inwardly at the graphic realism of the unfolding story but said nothing. Sad as it was, she suspected Emily had told this story before and took some measure of comfort in retelling it.

"Did you grow up here on the Cape?" asked Olympia.

"No. I grew up in Western Massachusetts, the northwest corner, in North Adams. It was a depressed area after the mills and the factories closed down, but since then it's become very desirable. I hear they even made a huge museum out of one of the factories there. I have no intention of ever going back, though. I don't even like to drive through it. Too many bad memories. What about you?"

Olympia knew to keep her own story out of this and thus answered minimally. "I grew up in the Boston area. Like you, I'm a New Englander. But tell me, is there something in particular that you came here to talk to me about?"

Emily looked down at the floor beside her and began chewing on her lip again. "There is, but I'm not ready yet. I need to think about how I want to say it. Can I come back later this week?"

Olympia reached for her date book. "I think next week would be better. I've found that we need time to think about what we say and hear in meetings like this, and to be honest, I don't do long-term counseling."

"What do you mean? Can't I come and see you after next week?"

Olympia smiled to reassure her. "Of course you can, but I want the best for you. I'm beginning to think this is a more deep-seated issue than what I'm trained to handle, and with your history, the last thing I ever want to do is the wrong thing. Surely you can understand that."

"I'm trying to. I get two visits with you, then it's out the door, right?"

Olympia recognized the manipulation and she didn't like it. She answered very carefully. "That's not what I said, Emily. I do want to hear about what's troubling you, and then together we'll talk about how we might approach dealing with it. If you need professional help, then I'll recommend someone. If not, then we talk about a way to help you feel more integrated here at Salt Rock while you work on it. Does that make sense to you?"

Emily nodded, and then she looked up at Olympia and smiled.

"It's so good to be able to talk to someone who gets it, Reverend. I don't think Reverend Rutledge likes women very much. No, I'll change that. He just didn't go to any trouble to get to know me. He was always too busy, and he played favorites, too. You had to be on his good side. Even after only one Sunday I can see that you don't do that."

Olympia did not change her expression. "We'll talk more next week, Emily. How about Wednesday? It makes more sense to be here when the administrator's in the office. That way we won't be interrupted by someone dropping in or the phone ringing."

"That sounds okay. You want me to bring you some coffee?"

"That's very kind of you, Emily, but I can make some right here if I need it. If you like, I'll even make some for you. Oh, and one more thing, thank you for the flower. It was wilted when I found it, but I cut back the stem, put it in some water, and it perked its little self right back up, see?"

"Just my way of saying thank you, Reverend. See you on Sunday, if not before." Emily smiled and left without another word.

Poor thing, thought Olympia, it's no wonder she's so desperate for attention. With a background like that, who wouldn't be? Over her years as a college professor, and more recently a parish minister, she'd encountered this kind of thing any number of times. Usually all that was needed was exactly what Emily said she wanted, help fitting into the community with a little support and recognition along the way. Olympia smiled to herself. She knew from experience it was wise to deal with this kind of thing early on before became it an issue. If ignored, such people would continue to grumble and whine at greater and greater levels of intensity, and eventually disruption, until someone finally took notice and reached out to them.

Nope, she was on top of this one. Thus satisfied she was on the right track, it was time to find some lunch. Eileen Sullivan would be there at one, and Olympia didn't want to be distracted by hunger. Surely there would be a coffee shop or neighborhood lunch place nearby where she could grab a quick bite and be back in plenty of time. Olympia pulled on her coat, snatched her keys off the bookcase and quick-stepped out to her car. As she did, something dark flashed overhead, and she heard the unmistakable 'cree-cree-cree' of a predator hawk.

Nine

Eileen was sitting in her car when Olympia returned to the church at ten minutes to one. Together they walked in through the main door, and even before they took off their coats, Olympia offered to make them a pot of tea. The casual informality of pottering about in the church kitchen, boiling water and finding cups, would ease the tension of what she knew was going to be a difficult conversation, however it played itself out.

Eileen nodded enthusiastically. "I'd love some; I got really cold sitting in the car. I didn't want to be late—then when you weren't here, I was afraid I'd missed you."

Olympia took Eileen's arm and steered her toward the kitchen.

"Whenever there's a problem at home," Eileen continued, "my mother always says, 'Let's start with a nice cup of tea. Then we'll think about what needs talking about, but tea first, and talk second."

"She sounds like a woman after my own heart," said Olympia, pulling open cabinet doors and looking for cups and spoons and, oh yes, the tea. "My Irish grandmother, and now my English husband, both consider a cup of tea the cure for pretty much anything that ails you."

"Almost anything," whispered Eileen, pressing her mouth with one hand and holding the other against her stomach.

Olympia placed her hand ever so gently on the young woman's shoulder. "Tea first, and talk second. We've got all afternoon."

Once they were settled in her office, Olympia sipped her tea and made general comments on the temperature and about the cruel wind outside until Eileen looked as if she was ready to talk.

"I did go to Planned Parenthood, and you were right about one thing."

"And that is?"

"They were really nice and took all kinds of time explaining things. They asked me if I wanted to see a chaplain before I made my decision, and they even gave me some hints on how to tell my parents."

"Are you going to tell your parents after all?" asked Olympia.

"No, that hasn't changed. I said I had a minister I could talk to. I didn't give them your name, though."

"You could have."

Eileen shook her head. "The fewer people who know about any of this the better, even down in Rhode Island."

Olympia nodded and waited.

"It's weird."

"What's weird?" asked Olympia.

"Yesterday when I called you, I was absolutely certain I was going to have an abortion. I even have the name and address of the place in my purse. But when they asked me if I wanted them to call and make an appointment, I said I wanted to do it myself."

"And have you?"

Eileen looked at the floor. "Not yet."

Olympia sipped her cooling tea and waited.

"I want to, and I don't want to, and it's not the Catholic thing either. I'm more or less clear on that. I don't know what it is. Yesterday I was sure I knew what I wanted to do, but now something feels different."

'It's an enormous decision, Eileen. I'm glad you have given yourself more time to think about it." Olympia was being very careful not to say anything about sin, human life or unborn babies, nothing that might even remotely influence the decision one way or another. The poor thing was in a terrible place, but chaotic as it was, at least she had options. When Olympia had been pregnant with her daughter, there had been only one option, and she'd had no choice but to take it. Her mother saw to that. Then she thought of her own daughter and the decision she had made and how she was dealing with it.

"Eileen, on Sunday you said there was no way on earth you were going to tell your parents. Are you sure you're still feeling that way? Do you think maybe you should rethink that decision?"

Her face crumpled, and it was a few minutes before she could speak, but she didn't answer the question.

"I know what I have to do. I'm just trying to get up the courage to do it, and I don't have much time."

"A couple of days isn't going to make that much difference."

Eileen put down her teacup. "I know this is a lot to ask, and you only met me two days ago, but I wonder if you'd consider going with me when I have it done. There's no one else I could even consider asking. I'd pay for your time."

"Of course." Olympia didn't have to think about her response. It was automatic. There was no question in her mind that she would do it, but whether she wanted to was a very different question. Damn!

"However, you absolutely will not pay me," she added.

"But …"

Olympia shook her head and held up her hand. "Being present is what I do. You just need to tell me when."

"Can I call you tomorrow morning and let you know?"

"Of course you can, and if you want to come in and talk again before you make the call, or even make it from here, you can do that, too."

"What time do you come in to the office, Reverend?"

Olympia thought fast. Jim was coming down that evening, and no doubt they'd all be staying up late.

"I plan to be here by ten. The administrator will be in, so if you don't want to be seen, you might want to use the side door."

"I don't know how to thank you," Eileen whispered.

"You don't have to thank me, Eileen. You are just letting me do what I am called to do."

"God didn't call you to shepherd wayward girls who walk in off the street. Isn't that a little above and beyond the call of duty?" Eileen was pulling on her coat.

"You aren't wayward, and you didn't walk in here by accident. There are no accidents. I believe coincidence is God's way of remaining anonymous. You came here for a reason that right now we are only just beginning to understand; but I, for one, am willing to let the purpose of all this be revealed in God's own time—not yours, not mine."

"Amen," said Eileen.

Olympia smiled. "Call me when you're ready."

When Eileen was gone, Olympia took herself out to the church kitchen for another cup of tea and to see if there might be anything munchable lurking in the fridge. She needed some contemplative quiet before switching gears into home and hearth mode.

Thirty minutes later she was buzzing up Route 6A, thinking about dinner and what she might serve with Jim's new favorite wine. She decided on one of their favorites, linguine tossed with great oozy chunks of warm brie, topped with chopped plum tomatoes and fresh basil. Add a bag of fresh salad and some hot bread to that, and they would have a meal to die for. She was getting hungrier by the mile.

Earlier in the day, Frederick worked at home to solve the problem of how to fill the opening he'd created in the wall of Olympia's future office. He was looking on line for windows when he realized that his lady wife might want to have the final say for a window, or windows, she was going to be looking through. Congratulating himself on such amazing and deferential foresight, he turned off the computer, made himself a cup of tea, opened his latest book and waited for the good reverend to come home. All in all, it had been a good day. Frederick Watkins was a happy man.

Sitting alone in her sea-blue and white bedroom, Eileen Sullivan was hugging the ragged one-eyed teddy bear she'd had since her first birthday. Her mother and father were downstairs in the living room. At the end of most days, they sat and enjoyed a glass of wine and shook out the tensions of the day before starting dinner. She could hear them talking, but they were too far away for her to make out the words. Eileen remembered doing much the same when she was little, feeling safe and comforted by the sound of their voices as she drifted down into sleep. But that was then and this was now, and she wanted mummy and daddy to make everything right the way they could when she was little.

She so wanted to tell them, to run downstairs and fly into their arms and have them push a button and make it all better. She was struggling with herself. If it were happening to her daughter, she'd want to know. My daughter. Maybe I'm carrying a girl, she thought. Then she changed her perspective and tried to imagine how she'd feel if one of them had a serious problem and kept it from her? That's when she realized no matter what the consequences, she had to tell them. Love, loyalty, respect and their long-held family values demanded no less.

Eileen set the teddy bear back in his accustomed spot on her pillow and smoothed her hair. Then she opened the door to her room and called down the stairs.

"Mum, Dad, have you got a minute?"

Ten

By the time Olympia pulled into the driveway, Jim and Frederick were already enjoying their first glass of wine. Her own glass would be waiting for her, covered in plastic wrap and chilling in the fridge. She hung up her hat and coat in the entryway off the kitchen, grabbed her wine and joined them.

Neither of them stood when she entered the room because both were fully "catted." She knew the fastidious Father Jim would be asking for a roll of masking tape to clean his trousers later, but for the time being he seemed quite content to let the hairy fluff accumulate.

"How was your day?" asked Frederick.

Olympia enjoyed a generous swallow of her wine before responding.

"Interesting." Another swallow. "Mmm, this is great, Jim."

The two men looked at each other. "Could you expand upon your use of the word interesting, my dear?" asked Frederick.

"When Dickens wrote *A Tale of Two Cities*, he called it a study in contrasts. Let's say my day could well be called a tale of two ladies, also a study in contrasts."

"And this," said Frederick, pointing to the animals, "could be called a t-a-i-l of two kitties."

Both Jim and Olympia gagged and then scored one for Frederick.

"Why don't we start again?" said Jim.

"I believe you both know that a young woman who is trying to deal with an unplanned pregnancy showed up at church on Sunday."

The two men nodded.

"Well, she came in to my office today. Poor thing, she's so conflicted."

"Has she made a decision then?" asked Jim.

"I don't think so. I'm convinced she really wants to tell her parents, but she's terrified of doing it. I know she's struggling with the whole Catholic thing on abortion, as well, but I know there's a whole lot more. I guess there always is. It would be easier if it were simply a case of right and wrong or yes and no, but … " She shook her head.

Jim smiled in sad, sweet understanding.

"Ah, yes, the Catholic thing … and you're right, it is so multidimensional."

"I honestly don't think abortion is the right thing for her."

"I thought you were totally pro-choice, Olympia. Having a change of heart?"

"Not at all. That's just it. It's her choice, and she's having one hell of a time trying to make it, but at least she has a choice."

"Does she know that?" asked Jim.

"I'm not sure, but I can't push her."

"Agreed," said Jim.

"Wasn't there another woman you were going meet with today, as well?" asked Frederick.

"There was, but that one's not going to be a problem. She has a background that would make anyone anxious and insecure. She just needs affirmation and boundaries in whichever order the situation demands, but we start with affirmation. She'll be okay. I've dealt with it before. Once she feels safe and accepted, she'll be fine."

As Jim raised his glass in Olympia's direction, the antique beehive clock on the mantel over the woodstove, the one that never worked without a reason for doing so, added an affirmative series of pings.

"There, now, Miss Winslow likes the idea, too. I say if anyone can help that woman to feel better, you can. You'd find something positive to say about the devil himself. Positive thinking is good medicine."

"Considering what her childhood was like, I think she's done amazingly well. That's what I'll build on. It just might take a while."

Ping.

"Sounds like you're on it, Madame. And now for something completely different, is it dinner time yet?"

"I picked up some beans and low-fat turkey franks to go with that new wine of yours. Maybe a side of ketchup?"

Jim almost choked on his five-star wine.

"Gotcha," said Olympia with an impish grin. "Then after dinner, along with dessert and coffee …"

"And brandy," interrupted Frederick.

"You can tell us your good news," finished Olympia.

Olympia knew that Jim liked a long build-up to his stories, and she was making sure he got full measure.

Eileen Sullivan walked slowly down the stairs and into the pleasantly cluttered living room. As was their custom at the end of the day, her parents were seated facing the oversized window, each holding a glass of wine and enjoying their private ocean view. At five o'clock they would have a second glass of wine and turn on the evening news. At six they would go out to the kitchen and start supper, or call for take-out, or make reservations at a local restaurant. They did this more and more now that all of their children except for Eileen were safely out of the nest.

Their time was their own, and they were making the most of it. John Francis Sullivan, Eileen's father, had gone so far as to cut back to four days a week and had handed the emergency pager off to the newest (and most eager) member of Lower Cape Cod Family Medical Associates, Inc. Their life was comfortable and predictable, and in the next ten minutes their youngest daughter was about to change all that.

Theresa Sullivan looked up and smiled as her daughter entered the room, but her expression quickly changed to one of apprehension.

"Whoa! Why the long face, sweetie. You look like you just lost your last friend. Want a glass of wine?"

Unconsciously Eileen put her hand on her abdomen and just as quickly snatched it away. "No, thanks, Mom, I'm fine."

She took the chair farthest away from her parents, an old wing chair which had been in her family for generations. "Actually, I haven't lost my best friend, but I do have something pretty serious I need to talk about."

Both parents, instantly concerned, put down their glasses and turned to their daughter. "What it is, honey, something at school?" asked her father.

"Is it the car, have you had an accident?"

"No, Mum, it's not the car, and no, Dad, school's fine. I'm still running at a 3.8 grade point average. This has to do with me, and I'm afraid it's not good."

"Well, don't just sit there, tell us. There's nothing so terrible that we can't fix or at least help you with. We're your parents, that's what we do. We make things better. We've always told you there was nothing in the world you couldn't tell us."

Eileen was twisting her fingers and staring at the floor, but she was not fighting back tears. "I'm not so sure about that, and I don't know how or where to start."

"Try the beginning," said her dad in the gentle voice he used with his patients when they were about to receive some difficult news.

Eileen lifted her chin and looked directly at her parents. "I'm afraid it goes against everything you've taught me, and I don't know which is worse, that I've disgraced the family or that I've shattered all the dreams you had for me. I've totally wrecked my life. I'm four weeks pregnant."

John Francis gasped, and Theresa burst into tears. Eileen remained dry eyed and sat ramrod straight in the chair, waiting as the barrage of questions tumbled over each other and flew past her head. Both her parents were trying to make sense of what they'd just heard. One by one, Eileen did her best to answer them in order.

"Of course I know who the father is, so do you. He's a good person. No, I don't want to marry him. No, he doesn't know, and I don't plan to tell him. By all calculations, mid-September. I have every intention of finishing college, and … I don't know."

Doctor Sullivan's commanding voice cut through the whirlwind of questions and suggestions.

"Eileen, Terry, stop. We have time."

"What are you talking about, John? She's pregnant, that isn't going to change. What kind of time are you talking about? We have to figure something out before she starts to show and people find out. I suppose she could transfer to another college for her last semester. Maybe …"

"For God's sake, Terry, shut up!" roared John Francis Sullivan.

Eileen held up her hand to speak.

"Excuse me, Mum, Dad, but this decision is mine to make, and I've made it."

Her father waved away any further words she might have wanted to say with a dismissive gesture. "Will you both stop talking and listen to me? Look, I'll have one of my colleagues in Boston, uh, take care of this, and no one will ever be the wiser. A day or two off your feet to rest, and you'll be right back to school, done and dusted."

Eileen couldn't believe what she was hearing. Every moral and religious value he'd ever espoused and instilled in her dissolved in the words "take care of this."

"Thank you, Dad, but you are not going to take care of this, as you so clinically put it. I'm of legal age, and whatever decision is to be made, I am going to be the one to make it."

"But …" sniffled her mother, her face blotchy from crying, her wine glass long forgotten.

Eileen leaned forward in her chair. Now her voice was beginning to quaver. "Dad? Mum? You have no idea how sorry I am this has happened. At first I wasn't going to tell you. Yesterday I drove to Rhode Island to an office of Planned Parenthood. I had every intention, as you put it, of taking care of it. "

"You need to talk to someone," interrupted her father. "I know about these things."

"I have someone to talk to."

"Who is it?" asked her mother.

"I'm not saying," said Eileen.

"So what are you going to do? When will you know?"

"I'm not saying, because I don't know. This afternoon, upstairs in my room, I thought I had everything worked out, but now I'm not so sure."

"When will you …?" They said it in unison.

"Dad, Mum, please. I'm not sure which of us is feeling the worst about this right now, but I told you because I trusted you. Now you have to trust me. If I have questions I think you can answer, I'll ask you. Right now I need time to think. Then, whatever I decide to do, I promise to tell you before I actually do it."

"But …"

Eileen stood up and started toward the door.

"If you don't mind, I'm going out. I need some fresh air. "

"It's dark. You shouldn't be out alone," said her mother.

"We have streetlights. I'm only going down to the All in One. It's a ten-minute walk. I'll be right back. I just need to clear my head. You want milk or anything?"

Both her parents shook their heads in stunned silence as Eileen pulled her coat and bright green scarf out of the front hall closet.

"Be careful, honey," whispered her mother.

"I just need some air. I won't be long."

Eileen stepped outside and pulled the door shut behind her. The night was clear and cold, very cold. As she walked along the familiar street she counted the houses that still had Christmas lights blinking in their windows. There were five, counting hers.

Eleven

Olympia, Frederick and Jim had plowed through every morsel of the linguini and brie concoction and were now sprawled contentedly in their respective chairs. They were sniffing and sipping at thimblefuls of the pricey cognac Jim had given them at Christmas when Olympia began tapping her foot.

"Okay, Jim, I've waited long enough. What's your big news?"

Jim smiled at his friend. "I'm looking into an adjunct position teaching world religions at the Episcopal Theological Seminary in Cambridge. It's only one class a semester, but it's a requirement, so it gets offered on a regular basis. I'd have a foot in the door, and it's an easy commute. I'm thinking of getting rid of my car and saving myself some money and aggravation. Parking is ridiculous in Boston and Cambridge, particularly in the snowy season."

"That's terrific, Jim," said Olympia.

He waved his hand. "Wait, there's more. I just learned I can stay in the apartment on Beacon Hill. My friend who owns it has decided to extend his present position for another year."

"More and better, but what about Allston College? You've been teaching there for donkey's years," said Frederick.

"To tell you the truth, I don't feel comfortable there any longer, so I've given them my notice. What was it you said earlier, Olympia, something about the Catholic thing? I think that may be part of it. Don't get me wrong. No one there has even hinted that I don't belong there. However, I'm an Episcopalian now. I love teaching, and I think I'll feel more grounded working at ETS, if I get the job."

"I see what you mean, Jim, but …"

"Wait, there's even more."

"I don't know if I can stand it," said Olympia. "I might need another slosh of brandy."

"It's called cognac, and one doesn't slosh cognac, one liberates it." Jim assumed an air of exaggerated superiority.

Frederick frowned in Olympia's direction. "You may have one ferocious headache if you do."

Olympia put a hand to her ear. "Am I hearing the soft, sweet voice of reason, husband mine?"

"You are, indeed, but I do believe Jim has one more shoe to drop. Am I right, dear boy?"

Jim smiled and nodded. "I've just accepted a half-time position as a chaplain at Mercy Hospital."

"How can I ever forget Mercy Hospital?" Olympia spoke with a tight smile. "I was almost killed there."

"So you were, but the man who did it is dead and buried. It will be great working with Wanda—I mean, Sister Patrick. We go way back."

"So this means …"

"I can support myself doing what I love where I want to do it."

"It can't get any better than that," said Olympia.

"Actually, it could, and only time will tell." A wistful smile. With that, Jim held up his glass and asked for a drop more cognac, adding, "If there's no objection, I think I should stay the night."

"You never have to ask, Jim. Your room is exactly as you left it, including the dust, and I'm assuming you still have your house key."

Eileen Sullivan was feeling better for her walk but dreaded going back into the house. Understandably, her parents would want more information, but she couldn't tell them anything more, because she no longer knew what was going to happen next. The ground was shifting under her feet, and she had nothing to hold onto. She stopped on the sidewalk outside her house and leaned back on the fence so she could look up at the stars and let the wonder of creation cast its magic spell, but it wasn't long before her neck began to hurt, and her toes and fingertips ached from the cold. She pushed off the fence, rubbed the back of her neck and started slowly up the front steps. There was no point in adding frostbite to her list of miseries.

In Brookfield Jim, Frederick and the cats had all gone to bed, and Olympia was sitting alone by the remains of the fire, holding a cup of chamomile tea. She was thinking about her daughter Laura and her granddaughter, little Erica. She looked at the clock that didn't work and was reminded that Eastern Standard Time was three hours ahead of California time. Maybe Erica would still be awake. Olympia reached for the phone beside her chair.

"Mom? Is everything all right?"

"I'm fine, and so are Frederick and the cats. I was just sitting here thinking about you and decided to give you a shout. How's the job, how's my granddaughter and, most importantly, how's my darling daughter?"

Laura chuckled. She had a low and pleasing voice. "Pretty good on all fronts, I'd say. I'm getting used to it out here. Erica loves her day care situation, which means I love it, and I can give my full attention to my work. They've got me on a new market research project which should keep me off the streets and out of trouble for a couple of months. It has to do with cross-generational electronic communication."

"Wow, I'm impressed. I'll be interested in the results."

"So will I, Mom. We're just starting to sketch out the initial research trajectory, which of course will lead to another and likely another after that."

"I'm lost already," said her mother.

"I'll let you know how it comes out, but don't hold your breath, okay? Do you want to speak to your granddaughter? She's trying to eat the arm of the chair. She's teething again."

There followed a few minutes of excited babble interspersed with words like "gamma," "goggie," several loud "no's" and an indignant screech when Laura finally retrieved the phone.

"Let me call you back when I get little miss drama queen into bed. There are a couple more things I want to run by you before I start making plans for the summer."

"Sure, sweetie. I'll be up for a little while longer. On the other hand, if time gets away from you tonight, you can call me tomorrow. I'll be here."

Olympia hung up the phone and reached for Miss Winslow's diary.

Reading this little book had become a kind of private time with a woman who had become a friend and perhaps even a curious a kind of protector/confidante. Leanna Faith Winslow was a woman who faced many of the same struggles over a hundred and fifty years ago that Olympia was dealing with right now. She'd had a child out of wedlock, a gay best friend, and like Olympia, she was searching for her rightful place in the world and the time in which she lived.

She smoothed her hands over the cover of the diary and then held it against her chest. For some reason it always felt warm, and therefore curiously comforting, to the touch. She thought about her house and the secrets it still held. I wonder what else I'll find in this place, she mused. We haven't gone through half the nooks and crannies yet, and now that I think of it, I seem to remember reading that this particular journal might not be the only one she kept.

Olympia leaned back and looked up at the clock on the mantel. She'd begun thinking of it as Miss Winslow's private line. Her affable house-ghost often used the clock to get people's attention. In fact, hadn't she ping-ed them all earlier that very evening?

Olympia smiled in pleasant anticipation as she opened the book to where she'd last left off. As she did so, a scrap of paper, yellow and brittle, fell into her lap. That's odd, she thought. I don't remember slipping anything in here. Curious to see what it might be, she picked up the paper and turned it over to find a few words written in Miss Winslow's distinctive hand: *This cold is deadly. I fear for the wild creatures of the night and more so what the morrow might bring.*

If there was a message in these cryptic words, Olympia was not getting it. She wondered, after three years of keeping custody of this precious book, how she could have missed the scrap of paper. On the other hand, by now she realized that Miss Winslow had her little ways. She tucked the scrap back into the diary, and would show it to Frederick and Jim in the morning.

February 6, 1863
I am stealing a few moments to write these few words.
We are having a most fearsome snowstorm, and our
poor Louisa has taken a turn for the worse. Her skin
is pale and damp, and her breathing has become quite
labored. We can't possibly go out for a doctor, so we
must try and care for her ourselves. Jonathan stands
at her door and waves at her when he sees that she is
awake. Such a sweet child. He has his father's
temperament ... and his father's eyes. He sees things
that are beyond his understanding.
More anon, LFW

Emily Goodale slipped into the pre-warmed double bed
with her latest romance novel. On cold nights like this, an
electric blanket turned up to high and a titillating book was
about as good as is it got for now. One day she'd find
someone to share that bed with her, she knew that. All in good
time, she told herself. Everything comes to those who wait. It
had been a good day. She liked that new minister, Olympia
Brown. She really listened and even offered to make coffee
for her instead of the other way around. Maybe there would
be a place for her in the Salt Rock Fellowship after all. Emily
wiggled down into the pillows, opened her book and smiled as
her thoughts drifted back to Olympia. It had indeed been a
good day.

Twelve

The next morning, Frederick, Jim and Olympia were seated at the kitchen table, picking and choosing from a clutter of breakfast foods before them. Frederick was nursing his customary oversized tea mug, while Olympia and Jim were savoring cups of fresh, hot coffee. The cats knew better than to interrupt this ritual and were curled, back to back, in the patch of sunlight flooding in through the kitchen window.

"So what are your plans for the day, Reverend Lady?" asked Jim.

"I said I'd be at the church by ten, so I should be on the road in about an hour."

"I say, do you keep a blanket in the car, Olympia?" asked Frederick.

"I do, but what in the world made you ask? It is a bit out of the blue, even for you, my predictably *nonsequitur*-ious Englishman."

"It's just that it's bloody cold out there. Look at the frost on the windows. On the best of days that van of yours can be temperamental. I'd hate to think about you being stuck somewhere and not able to keep warm. Actually, maybe you should think about replacing it ..."

Olympia held up her hand. "Don't even finish that sentence, my dear. I'll keep it until the wheels fall off, and it rolls over and breathes its last. You know how I feel about that thing."

"Only too well, but one of us should have a car that can be depended upon."

"May I interject a thought?" asked Jim.

"Be my guest."

"Do you remember my saying last night that I was thinking of getting rid of my car? Well, I don't really want to. There are times I'd really like to have one, but rentals can be expensive. Perhaps I could leave it here, and you two could have the use of it, and I could take it when I wanted or needed it."

"Capital idea, old boy," said Frederick.

"We certainly have the room," added Olympia.

"Consider it done. You can leave it off whenever you want."

"If one of you would take me to Braintree, I'll leave it and a set of keys today. That would be terrific."

Olympia looked at her watch. "I need to get a move on, but before I do I want you to see something I found last night when I was reading Miss Winslow's diary."

She stood, swallowed the last of her coffee, went into the sitting room to get the diary and returned with a very puzzled expression on her face.

"What's wrong?" asked Jim.

"It's not there. Last night a scrap of old paper fell out of the diary with the words, 'This cold is deadly. I fear for the wild creatures of the night and more so what the morrow might bring.' It was written in Miss Winslow's hand, and now it's gone."

"You were very tired last night. You don't suppose you dreamed it, do you?" asked Frederick.

Olympia shook her head. "No. Actually, I was quite wide awake. I'd just had a really nice long distance chat with my daughter and an even nicer babble with the baby. No, it was there, all right, and now it isn't."

Frederick reached for the teapot and poured himself half a cup. "Do you think it might be some sort of message or warning from Miss Winslow? She has been ping-ing about a bit these last few days."

"Might be, but what does it mean? The cold, wild creatures and the morrow, which is now today?" She shook her head.

"True, and we did just have a chat about the cold and taking care of yourself and having blankets in the car."

"And water and maybe some granola bars," added Jim. "We shouldn't take New England winters lightly just because we live in a well-populated area. Heck, I grew up in the middle of the city, and I remember times when we lost power for days at a time. I know it was dangerous, but we all would huddle around the gas stove in the kitchen. We even slept in there one night. It was scary."

Olympia was pulling on her coat and fumbling around in the pockets for her hat. "Don't worry about it now, we'll figure it out. It's undoubtedly about being careful out in the cold. I'll throw another blanket in the back of the van, and the water and the granola bars, Jim. But right now I need to be on the road. I'm expecting Eileen Sullivan at ten, and I want to be there and settled in before she arrives."

When the dust of Olympia's leaving settled, Jim and Frederick smiled across the table and toasted each other with their almost empty cups.

"That's our girl," said Frederick.

"I'm in no rush to get back today. If you want me to give you a hand with Herself's office project, I wouldn't mind getting my hands dirty."

"That's very kind of you, Jim. Olympia may or may not have told you that I sort of liberated a window space on the outside wall in that room, and at the moment, I do believe that it is far too frigid out there to make any meaningful progress."

"Ahhh," said Jim, which was immediately punctuated by a decisive ping-ping-ping, from the sitting room.

"Cup of tea, dear?" called Frederick.

The clock said nothing.

"Suit yourself," harrumphed Frederick.

Olympia pulled into the church parking lot at a quarter to ten. The drive had been uneventful, and spending the better part of an hour listening to public radio and enjoying the peace and tranquility of off-season Cape Cod was a lovely way to start the day. She wasted no time getting out of her car and settling into her office. She wanted to be ready for Eileen when she arrived, but ready for what? She told Charlotte she had a ten o'clock appointment and to please take any calls that came in.

Within minutes she heard a tap on her outside door and looked up to see a solemn-faced Eileen looking through the glass. Olympia pulled open the door and ushered her in out of the cold.

"Mother of God, it's cold out there," Eileen sputtered as she came in.

"When it's this cold, I worry about all the little wild things outside. I wonder how they keep warm and how many of them just die."

Olympia did a double take. What did she just say?

"You hear warnings all the time about taking care of your pets in weather like this. My two cats won't set a paw outside in this kind of weather. Say, do you need something hot to drink? There's tea and stuff in the kitchen."

"No, thanks. I'm feeling a bit queasy. I don't usually throw up, and it's usually gone by midmorning, so maybe in a little while."

Eileen pulled off her hat and coat and tossed them on a chair near the window before taking the chair she'd become accustomed to using.

Olympia smiled and waited. Eileen took a deep breath and blew it out slowly before speaking.

"I told my parents last night."

"What happened?"

"I guess it was pretty much what I'd expected, and at the same time it wasn't at all what I'd expected. The good part is that they didn't get mad. Shocked, yes, but not angry. My mother totally fell apart. Well, I guess they both did, but in different ways. She wanted to send me away, hide the whole thing and make up some stupid story about my taking a semester abroad. Right! More like no way in hell."

"What about your father?"

"He was all set to arrange a private abortion with one of his colleagues in Boston. I couldn't believe it."

"What couldn't you believe?"

Eileen paused and her eyes filled with tears. "My father is Mr. Super-Catholic. He's a good man, but taking care of it, as he put it, goes against everything he taught me to believe in four words: Take care of it. He wanted to 'take care of' his grandchild. The man I've looked up to and admired all my life turns out to be a total hypocrite."

Olympia considered her next words very carefully. "Is it possible that your father was feeling just as panicked and frightened as you've been feeling? He probably wanted to protect you from any further distress, and making it all go away is certainly one way to do it—only we both know it isn't."

Eileen nodded. "I hadn't thought about it that way."

Again Olympia waited before speaking. She was letting the silence between them have its rightful place in the conversation. To everything there is a time and a purpose under heaven, a time to speak and a time to refrain from speaking. Eileen was staring at the floor and twisting a tiny gold claddagh pinky ring on her left hand, and Olympia was refraining from speaking.

"I'm going to do it."

"Do what, Eileen?"

"I've decided I'm going to have the baby."

Olympia caught her breath. "Are you sure? What changed your mind?"

She hesitated. "It's probably the only thing I am sure of. I don't want to terminate the pregnancy, and it's not the Catholic thing either. My father blew that out the window last night. I have options, and they're my options. You and Planned Parenthood have helped me see that."

Olympia didn't dare ask the next question, but it must have been written across her face in block letters.

"I don't know yet, is the answer, but can I take you up on that offer of a hot drink now?"

Olympia was on her feet in an instant. "Of course you can. Come with me. We can scrounge around out there and see what we can find. I know there are some cocoa packets and some herb teas. Coffee on an empty stomach might not be the best thing. Oh, yes, and I do believe we have some saltines. They always worked for me when I felt queasy."

The two made idle chatter as they headed for the church kitchen. They spoke of the continuing cold, the age and simple beauty of the classic New England church and, more to the moment, what might they find to eat.

"When I was little my mother used to give me cocoa and saltines when I came inside from playing in the snow. I love the combination of salt and sugar together. It was worth getting frozen for."

Olympia was pulling open cupboard doors and rummaging around in the oversized refrigerator. Within minutes she managed to come up with several packets of instant cocoa, a half-full bag of oyster crackers and two giant mugs for their drinks, and she turned on the gas flame under the kettle.

Suddenly everything felt much closer to being normal. The awful tension of thirty minutes ago was gone. She didn't know what Eileen would do next, nor was she about to ask. Would she keep the child or give it up for adoption? Both were reasonable choices, depending on the desired outcome for the future of the mother and the child.

Olympia knew what she'd like to say, and she also knew there was no way in hell she would say it. It was not the time or the place to offer advice. It was the time to make cocoa and arrange some saltines on a plate for them both to share. She held out a steaming mug and the dish. "Take and eat all of this," she said. "Think of it as Unitarian Communion."

There was indeed, a time and a place for everything under heaven, and Olympia suddenly found herself profoundly and tearfully grateful.

"Come on, Eileen, let's go back to my office, where it's a little warmer. They keep the heat way down in here during the week. This place is like an icebox."

Thirteen

An hour later, when the cocoa and crackers were a pleasant memory, Eileen was gathering her things and making ready to go. She was still uncertain about what would happen in the long run, but now she had eight months to think about it. That, at least, was progress, and both she and Olympia were content for the time being.

When she was gone, Olympia stepped into the adjoining office to greet Charlotte and collect any messages that might have come in while she was in conference.

"One from Catherine Allen, asking if you could come to the board meeting next week, and one from Emily Goodale, asking if you were in. I said you were and asked if there was a message, but she said no and thanked me. That was it. I never know what to make of her."

Olympia was not about to sidestep an opportunity like the one which had just been presented to her.

"Really? How so?" She was the wide-eyed picture of innocent pastoral curiosity.

Charlotte shrugged her ample shoulders and turned both palms up. "She's new here. Well, new for a two hundred and fifty year-old church where half the families trace their roots back to the Mayflower." She wrinkled her nose. "How do I say it without sounding like a gossip? Mind you, I don't see her that much. I'm in here most of the time, but when I do see her it seems as if she's looking for something she can't find. Does that make any sense?"

It makes perfect sense, thought Olympia. "Maybe it's just her normal expression. I know some people who look like they're frowning all the time, but that's just the way their eyebrows work. It's disconcerting, though. I always worry that I've done something to offend them."

"I can say that she seems more relaxed since you came than she was with Reverend Phil," Charlotte continued. "Maybe that's just a man-woman thing. You know how some women get a crush on the minister. Well, it was just the opposite. I don't think she liked him. She never actually said anything, mind you, it was more an attitude thing. I see and hear a lot more in here than people realize because they think I'm part of the woodwork."

Olympia pulled up a chair and sat down. "I'll never ask you to break a confidence, but if there's something you think I should be made aware of, I hope you'll tell me. I'm only going to be here for a short time, and I want to leave the place as good as or better than it was when I arrived. It's what you do for a colleague, but it's more than that. It's my ministry."

"Phil Rutledge is a great guy, and I really like working with him, but I have to say that I know Emily got under his skin more than once. When she first joined the church, she was in here every other day, wanting something or other. But then something must have happened, because one day it just stopped. She came to church, but she wasn't dropping in here at all hours of the day anymore."

"I wonder what he said or did that changed things?"

"I wouldn't know, but whatever it was, it worked. Changing the subject, could you have the hymns and readings to me before you go home today? I need to get out the Sunday bulletin."

"Of course, Charlotte, and thank you for sharing what you did. I appreciate it. We ministers are not mind readers. People have to tell us what's going on, like who needs a visit or who's having a problem and needs a minister. You know the community, so I hope you'll be an extra set of eyes and ears for me."

"You bet," said Charlotte, "but I'll expect overtime for that."

"I'll do my best," laughed Olympia.

"By the way, if you don't mind my asking, who was that woman who came in earlier? She's not a member here, but her face is familiar."

"You're right, she's not a member. She's someone who asked to meet with me, and this seemed to be the most logical, private and convenient place for that to happen."

"Works for me," said Charlotte.

Olympia held up her index finger. "Now for something completely different. I'm starving. Care to join me for a sandwich somewhere close?"

"I can be talked into that. Have you a preference?"

"I'm new here, remember? I'm looking for cheap and close and not a franchise and where a vegetarian will find something besides pasta primavera."

"I know just the place. It's called The Green Revolution. A bunch of locavores started it up, and it's totally seasonal. In the summer they use all local produce and locally caught fish. In the winter they do fantastic things with winter vegetables and grains and such. All homemade breads and soups, too. It's great."

"Sounds perfect. I'll drive. That way I can find it by myself when you aren't here to guide the way."

When the two women returned from having their lunch, Charlotte closed up shop and left for home. Olympia decided to follow her example and call it a day, as well. It made much more sense to work on her sermon at home rather than to keep the building heated with only her there. Lovely and historic as it was, on a cold winter's day in January the creaks and rattles and groans of a historic building could be the teensiest bit disconcerting, even to Reverend Brave Heart Olympia Brown. Thus convinced, she collected her belongings, turned down the heat, locked and double-checked the doors, and left for home.

As she pulled out of the parking lot, she was already thinking of what they would have for supper, whether Jim would still be there, and what, if anything, her two favorite men had accomplished on what would one day be a home office. She needed to do a bit of shopping and stop in at the post office and the bank along the way, and it made sense to get it all done in what was left of the daylight. She was so busy with all of this, and so lost in the haunting sound of "Pie Jesu" from Fauré's *Requiem,* that she took no notice of the car behind her until she stopped for a red light. Only then did she recognize Emily Goodale waving, then signaling for a turn. Olympia waved back, and when the light turned green she tooted a greeting and stepped on the accelerator.

Emily waved again, turned right onto the beach road and pulled into a gas station. There she sat and watched Olympia drive north and out of sight. After making note of the time in a little notebook, she turned back onto the road and continued down to the shore and the far end of the town beach parking lot.

There she pulled a thermos out of her satchel and poured herself a steaming cup of heavily sweetened, milky coffee. She was due at work in less than an hour, and her custom, whenever she could manage it, was to take some quiet time by the sea. She would sit, sometimes with the car radio or a favorite CD playing in the background, watching the gulls wheeling and diving above the shifting tides. This was as close as she might ever get to a religious experience. It was here, not in church, where she found peace and forgiveness.

Church was good for being with people when she felt the need. She'd tried singles groups, and she'd tried taking classes and joining social clubs, but nothing ever quite worked. In truth, Emily was lonely. She didn't often dwell on why she never seemed to keep friends for very long or why some of the nicest people eventually turned away from her. That kind of thinking only made her feel defeated and even lonelier.

Then she pictured Reverend Olympia with her big open smile, those hazy green eyes, the short salt-and-pepper hair. She was so very welcoming. Emily leaned her head back against the headrest and watched as the now familiar image formed in her mind. Maybe this time she really had found the right place. God knows she'd tried out most of the other churches up and down the Cape without any success. Maybe things were finally turning around for her, and if they were, it was about time.

She looked at her watch. It was also time to get back on the road. The manager at the restaurant didn't like people to be late, and Emily couldn't afford to lose another job.

In Brookfield Jim and Frederick were closing up shop and considering which wine they would be opening for dinner. Earlier in the day Jim had suggested they cover the hole in the wall with a double layer of heavy gauge clear vinyl sheeting that would let in some reasonable light and at the same time block the winter winds. A side benefit of this improvement would be to retain enough heat from the electric radiator Frederick had picked up at a yard sale to allow the men to work out there without developing hypothermia. They were making progress. In the relative light and warmth of the long unused room, the two men cleared out years of accumulated detritus of who knows how many generations of Winslows and others who had been piling it up and leaving it for someone else to go through and clean out.

Much of it was junk, liberally besprinkled with dried-up mouse poop. Side by side they hauled out and bagged any number of boxes of old newspapers, bags of desiccated shirts and trousers, plus singles and pairs of dried-out leather boots and old-fashioned multi-buckled rubber galoshes. As they worked they speculated on the possibility of finding a hidden treasure or two, perhaps a Mayflower relic or an old Winslow family letter or document they could bring to the *Antiques Road Show*. They were well into the job when Frederick, who was digging through a particularly high and smelly pile of ancient clutter, scraped his hand on something sharp. Further digging revealed a rusty hasp, firmly padlocked, on a worm-eaten wooden sea chest.

"Blimey," said Frederick. "This has got some years on it. Come on, Jim, help me dig it out so we can take a look at it."

It took them a few minutes to get it clear of all the shreds and patches of other people's lives, but eventually they pulled it free and between them hauled it into the sitting room for further investigation.

"That thing is heavy. I wonder what's in it," said Jim, catching his breath.

"Lead weights or maybe cement building blocks,"

"Gold bullion, pieces of eight?"

"Dead bodies?" said Frederick in his best Basil Rathbone voice.

"No, Frederick, dead bodies wouldn't weigh anything by now."

"Fair enough. I'll go get a crowbar and pry it open."

Jim caught him by the arm. "Hold it right there, my friend. Unless you want to bring down the wrath of Olympia and all of Christendom on your freckled head, I suggest you table that idea until your lady wife gets in. I'm sure among the three of us we can come up with a way of getting it open that does not involve wanton destruction."

"You may have a point," said Frederick.

Ping, said the clock.

Frederick raised an imaginary glass in the direction of the mantel over the woodstove.

"I give up. I'm outvoted, two against one. Jim, how about you open some wine and make sure it is of the quality required. I'm in desperate need of a shower. Two to three hundred years of dust and mouse poop have turned me into part of the history of this place. A long hot shower will do wonders and bring me, without spot or stain, back into the present century."

"Just make sure you leave me some hot water. I'm just as gritted and begrimed as you are and more than ready to be rid of it." And to prove his point, Jim sneezed.

Fourteen

By the time Olympia came through the door, Jim and Frederick were washed and dried and discussing the merits of the wine Jim had so helpfully opened.

"Red or white, my love?" asked Frederick, removing a cat and levering himself out of his chair.

"Would you believe I'd like a cup of hot tea first, then I'll get on to the more serious stuff. It is really cold out there, and we all know how wonderfully warm my van can be on days like this. I lost count of my toes just after I crossed the bridge, and I checked just before I came in to see how many fingers I had left."

"Right-e-o, my dear. Herb or Rosie?"

"Herb please, it's way too late for Rosie."

"What in the world are you two talking about?" asked Jim.

"Ahhh, said Frederick with a knowing nod. "It's the secret language of the newly married, a heady cross of Cockney rhyming slang and Geordie colloquial."

"Of course," said Jim.

"Let me try and explain. Herb, said like the name, not pronounced minus the H, refers to an herbal tea, most often not containing caffeine. Rosie is short for Rosie Lee, which is rhyming slang for cup of tea, meaning the potent sludge we Brits were weaned on."

"I'm not feeling edified yet."

"How about a different approach then?"

Olympia threw up her hands in defeat. "Cease, Frederick. I'll make my own goddamn tea, because if I wait for you to explain it, I'll continue freezing to death, and none of us will have any supper."

"Sorry, love, I can get carried away sometimes."

"No kidding," muttered Olympia.

"Come again?"

"Really, Frederick, not in front of Jim."

By now Jim was completely confused but laughing with it. Frederick was heating the kettle, and peace and harmony were once again restored in the Brown-Watkins home.

The general merriment and camaraderie continued over dinner as the three of them went over the events of the day, and it was only when they went into the sitting room that Olympia spotted the sea chest.

"Whoa! Where did that come from?" And then to answer her own question, "Don't tell me you found it in the back room?"

"We did indeed. I even scraped my hand on it, see? Battle scarred in Milady's honor." Frederick held up his hand for Olympia to admire.

"What's in it?"

"We don't know. It's locked, and we don't have a key." Jim pointed to the rusty padlock clamped through an equally rusty iron hasp. "Your Frederick wanted to unseat said lock with a crowbar, but I suggested that among the three of us, we might be able to devise a way to access the inside without destroying the exterior."

"Or ringing for a locksmith," added Frederick.

Olympia did not roll her eyes. Rather, she walked around to the back side of the chest and pointed to the scrolled hinges. "Does anyone have a screwdriver? I think that and a bit of WD-40 might just do the deed."

"Of course," said Jim for the second time that evening. "Why didn't we think of that?"

"Because you're guys. You know, slash and burn, rape and pillage, and if it resists, beat it to death with a stick, or in this case, a crowbar. Women take a gentler, more persuasive approach. Frederick, go get me a screwdriver and some lubricant and a flashlight, and let's see what we can do with this thing."

It took a bit of convincing, but they managed to remove the hinges on the back and lever the top up far enough to aim the flashlight and peek inside. From what they could see, the chest was filled with bundles of papers tied with string, assorted record books or ledgers of some sort, and something that, in the darker shadows of the interior, looked like a metal box. A box within a box. Whatever could that be? It went without saying that Olympia was literally quivering with curiosity. If she were a cat, her tail would be twitching, and she would be chittering in anticipation. Because she had the smallest hands, she was elected to seize and lift out whatever she reached. Frederick held the flashlight, which he insisted on calling a torch, and Jim carefully held up and steadied the wooden lid. Olympia held her breath, eased her hands into the musty interior of the trunk and carefully pulled out the one thing that would fit through the opening. It appeared to be a ledger. She set it down on the coffee table, and Jim pulled a floor lamp closer so they could all see as Olympia lifted the dark green cover. She immediately recognized the firm and graceful hand of Leanna Faith Winslow, listing items purchased, repairs seen to and items disposed of, all carefully set down in orderly columns with dates and amounts paid.

"O-M-G," was all she could say.

"Blimey," added Frederick.

And Jim, who almost never swore, said, "Hot damn!"

Olympia was all but levitating, she was so excited. "Going through this is going to take some time, and I'm going to relish every word and page of it. I feel as if another window has opened on the life of my beloved Lady Leanna."

"Well don't get started on it tonight, or you'll never get up for work tomorrow," advised the occasionally practical Frederick.

"Much as I want to dive right into it, you're right. I'll keep it with the diary and save it for when I'm not cross-eyed with fatigue. This has been quite a day, and I'm going to bed."

The following morning, while they were all having breakfast, Olympia remembered to give Jim and Frederick the latest update on Eileen Sullivan. As Jim so wisely pointed out, she'd traded one desperate situation for another. The whole issue of whether or not to keep the child or give it up for adoption was equally as wrenching as the decision to continue or terminate the pregnancy.

"You're not telling me anything I don't know, Jim." Olympia was working her way through her second cup of coffee and trying to keep Cadeau from jumping into the middle of her breakfast. "I think a lot will depend on how her parents react. I suppose that will be the next chapter. There's no doubt I'll be hearing from her before long. Poor kid. I know how she feels. On the other hand, maybe I don't. I didn't have options."

Frederick reached for Olympia's hand. "No, you didn't, my love, and that was awful. But now you have reconnected with your daughter, and that's what really matters, isn't it?"

Olympia smiled sadly. "And she's in California."

"But you know exactly where she is," said Jim. "Four years ago you couldn't have said that."

"I'm sorry. Guess I'm having a little wallow. I think dealing with Eileen has brought up a good deal more old baggage than I thought was still in there."

Jim reached for her other hand. "You don't get over what happened to you. No one does, and if they say they're over it, they are in denial. When you have an emotional earthquake in your life, you eventually stumble past it and go on, but you never forget that it happened. I still think about Paul, and sometimes I find myself weeping over something that sparked a precious memory; but I have moved on just as you have, Olympia."

There was nothing to say after that, so the three friends sat, each lost in thought. Such was their mutual trust that this was possible.

The telephone broke the silence, and Olympia, who was the nearest, got up to answer it; but when she picked up the phone, the line was open, but there was no one there. Olympia shrugged and replaced the handset.

"Must have been a wrong number," said Jim.

"'Unknown caller' came up in the message window, and it's a little too early for telemarketers, so I'll go with Jim and assume it was a wrong number. Now that I'm up, I should probably get out of here. I'd planned to work on my sermon last night, but with all the excitement of finding the trunk, I didn't give it a thought. Duty calls, and it will be quieter and less dusty in the office than it will be here. Are you two going to continue the assault on the back room?"

Jim shook his head. "I've got to be back in Boston by midday. I'm happy to leave my car here, but I'll need a ride to the bus or the train. With the chaplaincy thing starting up, I'm going to be keeping more regular hours than I ever have done in the past. It's going to take some getting used to."

"I'll take you, Jim. I need to go to the building supply store, and it's not a mile away from the bus stop."

"What about the teaching thing at ETS, Jim? When will you hear about that?" asked Olympia.

"I'm not sure, but you two will be the first to know. That would give me just enough to get by and enjoy the odd bottle of good wine."

"Or the good bottle of odd wine," quipped Olympia.

"When I get back I am going to do some more in that room, but I won't touch the trunk until you get home. I put a few squirts of WD-40 into the padlock before I went to bed last night in hopes that in time it might be persuaded to give up its death grip on the hasp."

"Good thinking, noble husband."

"I'm not just a pretty face," said Frederick.

"You had me fooled."

"Olympia!"

She was pulling on her heavy coat and hat in preparation for braving the elements. "See you this afternoon, my love, and see you whenever, Jim. Good luck at Mercy hospital, and do give Sister Patrick my love. I think that will be terrific for all concerned—a match made in heaven for sure."

"I wouldn't go that far, but it will put food on the table."

Olympia was waving from the back door. "I shouldn't be late, Frederick. I'd rather not be driving on those twisty back Cape roads in the dark. They can be slippery when you least expect it. I'll be glad when it warms up a little. This arctic blast is a killer."

"It's all part of life's rich pattern, my love."

"Bag it, Frederick. It's bloody cold out there, and my van is like an igloo on wheels."

"Olympia, stop being such a martyr, and take my car. It's got a great heater, a terrific sound system and a brand new set new tires."

"What a good idea, Jim. Where are the keys? It's going to feel like driving a Tonka toy after driving my van, but the thought of warm feet is an offer I can't refuse."

Jim held out the keys. "She's old, but she's steady. Not good in snow, though. Cold or not, if you have to drive in snow, take the van."

"I wish it would snow. Then it wouldn't be so damn cold."

"Be careful what you wish for," said Frederick, the pessimist.

"I'm a New Englander, Frederick. Snow is in my DNA."

"Still …"

"See you tonight, dear. I don't have anything on my schedule other than the sermon, so I should be home early. Thanks again, Jim. I can't wait to experience driving and warmth at the same time. I don't know if my heart can stand it."

Fifteen

I could definitely get used to this, thought Olympia as she buzzed along the highway toward the Bridge. For the first time since she had fallen hopelessly in love with Volkswagen buses, and that was decades ago, she was driving in winter, and she was toasty warm. This kind of luxurious self-indulgence called for fresh coffee, and there just happened to be a drive-through place along the way. A nice, hot double cappuccino with cinnamon would be just the thing to complete the picture.

When she arrived at the church, she parked Jim's car in the spot marked Reserved for the Minister, double checked that the lights were off and the door was locked, and entered the building through the front door. Charlotte, wearing shades of blue today, was already ensconced at her desk, and as Olympia passed by she gave her a happy wave and held out a fresh blueberry scone.

"Be still my heart," said Olympia, reaching for it. "Did you make it?"

Charlotte laughed and shook her head. "Hardly. That Green Revolution place we went to yesterday has a bakery on the other side. Let's just say I'm a frequent flyer."

"Any messages that I need to respond to?"

Charlotte shook her head, "Quiet as a tomb. They don't call this the off season for nothing. That's why Reverend Phil decided to take his sabbatical now rather than in the spring or fall. Things start to ramp up around here by the end of April, and he likes to be on board when it gets busy."

"We're in different clergy groups, so we've never had a chance for a real conversation. I can tell you that this place has a healthy feel to it. I've been at this quirky business long enough to be able to say that and know what I'm talking about."

"I like it here. The people are nice. Of course, there are always one or two that take up a little more air than is really necessary, but eventually they fit in, or they leave."

Olympia nodded, her mouth full of blueberry scone. "Same the whole world over. Every so often one of the malcontents wreaks a little more havoc than necessary, but a healthy congregation can usually ride it out. Now it's time for me to tackle that sermon."

Outside, Emily Goodale drove slowly past the front of the church. She had the day off and was looking to see if Olympia was in yet. She was surprised and then dismayed to see, not a vintage blue VW van, but an older model grey Toyota Corolla, parked in the minister's space. When the strange car was still there after a third pass by, she turned into the parking lot, drove around to the back and parked safely out of sight. From her hidden vantage point she could see that a light was on in Olympia's office. How could that be? Who could it be? There was only one way to find out.

Emily switched off the engine, slipped out of her car and walked quietly up to where she could look into the office window without being seen herself. There she was, seated with her back to the window, working on her laptop. Why would Reverend Olympia drive a different car? Maybe it was because she didn't want people to know she was there. Emily could understand that. There were lots of times that she preferred to keep to herself. Maybe she'd ask about it next Tuesday. Emily stood and watched Olympia working for a few more minutes before climbing back into her car and driving away, but not before she'd memorized the license plate number on the Corolla.

On the other side of the country in San Jose, California, it was three hours earlier and fifty degrees warmer. Olympia's daughter, Laura Wiltstrom, was getting ready for work. Gerry was playing peek-a-boo with little Erica while Laura made lunches and filled the daycare bag for her daughter. Laura could not remember feeling so contented and so happy. This wasn't bouncing-off-the-wall happy or delirious-mindless-doing-stupid-things-happy, this was good-solid-feet-on-the-ground happy. Normal happy. She smiled over at Gerry and Erica and then crossed the kitchen to where they were sitting. She planted a big fat kiss on both their foreheads.

"When do we start telling people?" asked Gerry.

"Never mind when, my dear. First we have to decide what we are going to tell people, don't you think?" said the ever practical Laura.

"So what *are* we going to tell people? Work place romances are totally frowned upon. You know that."

Laura turned and faced her ladylove with a butter knife in one hand and a slice of whole wheat bread in the other. "Now that you ask, I guess I don't know. It's not as if we work in the same section or one of us is the other's boss or project partner. What's the rush anyway?"

Gerry switched from peek-a-boo to patty cake as she pondered what to say next.

"I suppose if anyone asks, we say we decided to move in together. Is it really anyone's business?"

"No it isn't, but it isn't anything I want to hide either, and more than that, I don't want to be the subject of office gossip and speculation."

"That's my woman," said Gerry

"Amen to that, girlfriend, and when that I think about it, we should probably start with our parents."

Gerry gave Erica a loving pat on the seat of her diaper and sent her scampering off toward her mother. "Gee, I never really thought about it until right now, but when did you first learn you were adopted, and what was it like meeting your biological mother?"

Laura smiled at the memory. "I knew from day one that I was adopted, or more realistically, from the time I could understand what that meant. My parents always told me I was their chosen one. They used to tease me and tell me they had the pick of the litter, and they took the best one."

"Well, what about Olympia? When did you meet her? That must have been weird."

"It's a long story, Gerry, and one I look forward to telling you and my daughter, but we need to get our butts out the door. If you'll grab the lunches and the baby gear and go out and start the car, I'll give herself here a swipe with a facecloth and get her jacket. I'm still not used to this kind of warmth in January. I wonder if I ever will be?"

The remainder of Olympia's day was uneventful. Thoughts of Eileen Sullivan kept flitting around the edges of her thinking and unsettling her. She knew full well there was nothing at all she could do, but it remained a concern and therefore a minor deterrent to the sermon, which she decided to call, "Coming In Out of the Cold." Eventually, jaw clenching, dogged persistence won out, and the thing began to take shape.

The other thought which kept intruding on her sermon process was the sea chest and its mysterious contents. She'd seen the ledger, and with it as a reference, she might be able to learn a lot more about the life and times of woman who'd lived in the house a hundred and fifty years earlier—and appeared to be sharing it in the present day, as well. She wondered what else they would find in there. More of Leanna's writings? Maybe some of her stories. That would be more than wonderful. Then she wondered if Frederick had been successful with the rusty old lock.

"That's it," she said to the computer. "I can't stand it anymore. I'm out of here."

Charlotte had already left, and Olympia wasn't overly fond of being alone in the echoing old place. When it was full of people, it was historic; but when she was the only one there, it was creepy. For the life of her, Olympia couldn't say why that was so, but it was.

Within minutes, she had locked up and was back in a rapidly warming little grey car and thinking of England. Olympia Brown was a happy lady. She was warm, and she was going home to a man she loved and a house she loved that had just offered up one more secret treasure for them to explore together. She whispered a prayer of thanks to the passing trees and the pale blue sky overhead and to anyone else that might be listening and headed straight for home.

That same afternoon, as the light was beginning to fade, Emily returned and once again parked in her secret spot behind the church. She considered waiting until the evening when the Ladies Alliance had their monthly supper meeting and slipping in then, but she thought better of it. She didn't want anyone to see her. A surprise is only a surprise when nobody knows about it.

She slipped out of the car walked around to the door that opened directly into the minister's office, took out her key and let herself in. It was still light enough to see her way to the desk, where she placed a gaily wrapped mini-box of chocolates along with a cream-colored envelope. It hadn't taken her long to learn that Olympia had a sweet tooth, and Emily was so grateful that she cared enough to really listen to her. A thank you card and a little box of candy was the very least she could do to show her appreciation. Wasn't it?

When the supper dishes had been stacked in the cupboard, and the cats were passed out in front of the fire, Frederick and Olympia were still laying siege to the padlock on the front of the trunk. Frederick, time and the trusty WD-40 had done their work. There was now fractional movement but not total access. They could always give in and call a locksmith, but Frederick did enjoy a challenge. He'd gone so far as to do a little internet research on antique locks and keys, and he was hopeful, now that the parts were moving, that with time and patience, they might indeed achieve the desired result.

"You know," said Frederick, armed with an ice pick and a small screwdriver, "there is always the chance that whoever locked this trunk may have hidden the key somewhere in that room. That would be logical, would it not?"

Frederick didn't often get high marks for being logical, but Olympia had to admit he had a point. More to that same point, why the hell hadn't she thought of it?

"I'm not planning on going in to the church tomorrow, so why don't I take some time poking around out there myself? I think I'd enjoy that."

Ping ping ping!

In one motion, the two turned in the direction of the clock.

"You see, she agrees with you, but now that I think about it, the dear old girl was making one hell of a racket this afternoon, clanging and boinging to beat the band, so to speak," said Frederick.

"Really? When was that?"

"I must say she certainly has developed quite a vocabulary for herself. Little pings generally mean she's content, boings and clangs mean she wants us to pay attention, and actual movement, of either the hands or the whole clock, means danger."

"Remember the time we found her face down on the floor?"

"I'd rather not, thank you," said Frederick.

"So back to this afternoon, Frederick. Exactly when was she making all the racket?"

"Let's see. The sun had set, but it wasn't yet dark, so four-thirty-ish."

"Hmm, the exact same time I was nice and warm driving home in Jim's car. I wonder what that was all about."

Frederick leaned over and patted her hand. "I trust that in the fullness of time, all will be made clear."

Olympia rolled her eyes. "If you don't mind, I prefer a more direct approach." With that, she reached for Miss Winslow's diary and held it up for him to see. "As you well know, I've often found that the words this dear lady wrote all those years ago provide me with insight and understanding into what is happening in my own life today."

"I've long since ceased to wonder at such coincidences," said Frederick.

Boing, said the clock.

February 10, 1863
Finally we have some sunshine, and how welcome it is. To everyone's surprise, Aunt Louisa survived the terrible influenza, but she is now quite frail. There is no question of her returning to Cambridge. We both

know it, but we didn't speak of it until today. She was having a good day, sitting by the fire, enjoying a second bowl of soup and watching Jonathan and Sammy. When she caught me watching her, she spoke in a low voice and told me she was ready to go. At first I didn't understand. "Back to Cambridge?" I asked. But then she said, "I've had a wonderful life, Leanna. You and Jonathan, and now Richard, have seen to that. You have given me a family, a second home, and now a place to say goodbye in peace and comfort. Do you know what a blessing that is?"

I tried a second time to protest and say she was much improved, but she was not fooled. I shall never forget her words. "Life begins, and life ends, Leanna. For everyone. You brought Jonathan into the world in my care, and now I shall leave this world in yours. I can ask for no more." Then she shut her eyes and rested for a few minutes before speaking a second time. "Everything will come to you and Jonathan; I revised my will before I left Cambridge."

After that she sat and rested in the warmth of the fire. Then she asked to be helped to her bed. I looked in on her before sitting down to these words and found her fast asleep, breathing easily and smiling.

More anon, LFW

Sixteen

The next morning, after a leisurely breakfast, Olympia knew that if she started prowling around in the back room, she'd never get back to her sermon. The key search and ancillary treasure hunting would be her reward for finishing the damn thing. After that, a lovely cool pale glass of wine and a nice hot pizza. On Fridays Frederick put in a full day at the bookstore, and they often enjoyed take-out or a restaurant meal as a wind-down from the week. Thus armed with good intentions and an oversized mug of fresh coffee, Olympia seated herself in the corner of their bedroom. As she did so, she let her thoughts meander forward in time to when she would have a real home office, a room of her own with a door and a huge window. A room where even the cats would have to ask permission to enter.

She was startled out of future time by the trill of the telephone on her desk. Not too many people other than family or Jim called her during the day, so it was with some pleasure that she answered.

"Hello? Hello?"

Nothing—no busy signal, not even heavy breathing.

Once again, the same as before, she could hear that the line was open, but there was no one on the other end. Olympia shrugged and hung up. It was probably a telemarketer, and the robo-call mechanism hadn't kicked in fast enough. Never mind, if it happened again she'd let the machine pick it up. As it turned out, she didn't have long to wait. Within fifteen minutes, not half enough time to get really into the task at hand, the phone jangled again. This time she sat and stared at it until she heard her daughter's voice.

"Mum, it's me. Give me a call when you get in, will you? I have some good news."

Olympia snatched up the phone. "I'm here. I thought you were a telemarketer."

"Gee, don't they usually call later in the day, like mealtime?"

"Never mind, what's your good news? I know, they made you president of the company."

"Better than that, Reverend Mother, and perhaps a bit of a revelation. You've heard me talk about my friend Gerry often enough. Well, we've moved in together. We've decided to be a couple."

Olympia hesitated briefly. "Wow. That's terrific."

"Why the hesitation?' Do you have a problem with that? You, of all people?" There was a quick, hard edge to Laura's voice, and Olympia could just see her standing in her kitchen, one hand on her hip and her chin thrust up and out.

"Not hardly, daughter mine. I just wasn't expecting it, that's all, and having been caught off guard, I was registering surprise. Have you told your other mother?"

Now it was Laura's turn to hesitate. "Uh, no. I'll be calling her next. She's a little more conservative than you and Frederick are, and I thought, well ..."

"That you'd practice on me." Olympia was smiling from ear to ear. In that moment of truth she realized she'd finally earned the trust she'd thought she might never have. Tears welled up in her eyes and spilled over onto her cheeks, and it was a struggle to keep her voice steady, but she willed it to be so. Her daughter was still talking.

"Now that I think of it, yes, I was practicing. I didn't think you'd be bothered, not with Jim for a best friend, but well, I guess I was afraid it might be different when it's your own flesh and blood. You know, like a variation on NIMBY, Not in My Back Yard."

"Laura, like every mother in the world, I want you to be happy and fulfilled in your life. If Gerry is part of that, if she loves you and Erica, and the three of you want to be a family, more power to you. I'll do everything I can do to support you all. So when do we get to meet her?"

"When's the next plane?"

Olympia laughed. "Not so fast, kiddo. I signed a three-month contract with a church on the Cape. I can't do anything until that's finished. I won't be free for at least ten weeks, but that will give us time to think and plan. Maybe we can come out for Easter."

"That might work. Then we'll have time to get the place ready for guests."

"Let me know when you've told your other mother. I won't say anything to anyone until then."

"You can tell Frederick and Jim."

"Okay, maybe just those two. They'll be very happy for you."

"Mum?"

"Yes, honey?"

"Thank you." It was a whisper.

"I want you to have joy in your life, Laura, and it sounds like maybe it's starting to happen."

It took Olympia a few minutes to catch her emotional breath after the phone call, so she wisely allowed herself a few minutes of staring into middle space and mindless cat-patting before returning to her sermon. The day was still hers, and the glow she felt because of her daughter's happy news would shine through and around everything she planned to do. With that she eased an unwilling feline onto the floor, did her best to ignore the pitiful yowl of abandonment and set to work.

On the street outside Olympia's home, Emily Goodale was doing a second drive-by. This time, she slowed down long enough to snap a picture of the house and the two cars, the van and Jim's Toyota, before turning around and heading back down to the Cape. She had to be at work by noon today, and there were a few things she needed to do.

Olympia hadn't been long at her sermon when the phone rang for a third time. She sat waiting, until she heard the caller leaving a message and recognized the voice of Eileen Sullivan.

"Hello?"

"Reverend Brown?"

"Good morning, Eileen, how are you doing?"

"Oh, up and down. I guess that's to be expected. I wonder if I could come up and see you."

"Of course. Let's see, today's Friday, I could see you Sunday afternoon after the service or Monday at eleven. Tuesday is going to be rather busy. Have you had a chance to talk with your parents yet?'

"Uh huh. I guess that's why I'm calling. I know they mean well, and they want to help me, but they can't do anything until I make up my mind. The minute I think I have, then I change it again, and forget about my studies. I can't put two thoughts together right now."

Alone in her room, the telephone held to her ear, Olympia smiled a sad smile of understanding and compassion. She knew exactly what this poor young woman was going through. She understood the choices and the obstacles and challenges that accompanied both of them. Of course, she would do what she could, which was listen. No advice, not a word of it, just be present.

"Eileen?"

"Yes?"

"What time do you go to mass on Sunday?"

"If I go, it will be the early one, why?"

"I'm thinking you might get something out of the sermon. I'm calling it "Coming in Out of the Cold." Our service starts at half past ten."

"Thank you. I think I'd like to hear you speak. When I came in that first time, I waited until everyone had left the church."

"I remember."

"Do I have to tell you if I'm coming?"

Olympia laughed. "Goodness no, we don't take attendance or ask people to punch a time card. Dress is pretty casual, and some people even bring their coffee or their knitting."

"Wow."

"Let's put it this way, you'll be welcome if you come, and if you can't come, you'll be just as welcome on Monday. I'll have the coffee ready."

Eileen made a strangled sound. "Ugh. No coffee, please. Since, well, um, I can't even bear the smell of it. Thanks anyway. Maybe I'll bring some tea or some cocoa. I've been absolutely craving chocolate."

"Comes with the territory," said Olympia.

"I suppose."

Olympia winced, wished her well and said her good-byes.

"Sermon or bust," she said to the cat, who had taken up residence on the pile of papers next to her computer. Cadeau flicked one ear in her direction, yawned and resumed his nap.

Later that day, Eileen Sullivan and her parents were sitting at the kitchen table. Each of them wanted to say the right thing, and none of them knew where to begin. Her mother had wiped and polished every flat surface in the room, and even now, rather than speak, she kept finding reasons to jump up and do or fetch something else. She was a bundle of nervous energy with nowhere to use it.

"Are you absolutely sure this is what you want to do?" Eileen's mother was the first to break the silence and address the issue head on.

"It's about the only thing I am sure of." Eileen was staring down at the table and tracing invisible patterns on the smooth wooden surface. "I'm still not sure whether or not I want to try and raise the child myself or place it for adoption."

Her father cleared his throat. His voice was tight, and it was clear he was having trouble finding the words. "Well, if you do decide to keep it, you wouldn't be raising it by yourself now, would you? You have a big family, and there's no question but we'd support you. I guess my question is, do you really want to limit your options by starting any kind of a career as a single mother? Lovely as they are, children are a responsibility that doesn't ever go away."

Eileen raised her head. "I know you're right, and I also know there are hundreds of people out there who would do anything to have a healthy baby, assuming this one will be healthy."

"With proper prenatal care, which I can personally guarantee you'll have, there's no reason why it shouldn't be," said her doctor father.

"You have time," said her mother.

"I need to decide before I can feel movement."

"Why is that?" asked her mother.

"I don't know whether or not this makes any sense, but it does to me. If I'm going to keep the baby, then I'll think about it as a mother; but if I know I'm going to place it for adoption, I'll try and see myself as a surrogate and maybe not get so attached. The people at Planned Parenthood told me if I do decide to give up the baby, I can even meet the future adoptive parents, and they might help with the medical expenses. Sometimes the adoptive parents are even present for the birth."

"I don't know if meeting the future parents would be a good idea. What if you changed your mind at the last minute and decided you wanted to keep it?"

"The baby, Dad, not 'it.' I'm having a baby, and whatever he or she might be, even now I can't think of this being as an it."

"I'm sorry, honey," said her dad. "Maybe you should go and talk to the people at Planned Parenthood again. I'm afraid we might be too close to you and the situation."

"I thought about that, Dad, and I think I'm going to go back and talk to a lady minister I've been seeing. I told you I was talking with someone."

"Will you ever tell us her name?" asked her mother.

"Eventually I will, but right now, for reasons I can't explain, I feel better not telling you."

"It's just that I'd like to be able to thank her for helping you."

Eileen looked across the table and tried to smile.

"You'll get the chance, Mum, just not yet, okay?"

With her sermon done and lunch firmly under her belt, Olympia set off to rummage around the back room on her own. No cats, no Frederick, no Jim, nothing on God's green earth to distract her. Before eating she'd gone out and turned on the electric heater so that by the time she started work, the room was cool but bearable as long as she kept her sweater buttoned.

With so much junk already cleared out, the room looked bigger than she'd remembered. Frederick said he'd measured it, but she decided to walk off the measurements for herself using a twelve-inch stride. It was ten feet by twelve feet or thereabouts with the longer wall on the outside, the one with the plastic-covered hole in it that would one day be home to two lovely crank-out windows. Light was important. Natural light energized her spirit and lifted her soul. A room with a view of the trees and birds and little wild things outside would give her endless hours of enjoyment. She promised to get bird houses and feeders and install them in the trees outside her future windows. Stop daydreaming, Olympia and get cracking.

The first order of business was to try to find the key. What a bummer is was to have the lid up just enough to see what was inside, but not high enough to get much of anything out. If this failed, and they couldn't pick it open, then she might give in and let Frederick take a hacksaw to it. The lock was old and lovely in its rusty, utilitarian way, but if push came to shove, she'd happily sacrifice an antique lock to get into that goddamn trunk. Curiosity was killing her. She needed to find that key.

She tried looking for a nail stuck in a bit of door frame or what was left of the window frame (not much) that had or might have at one time had a key hanging on it. Olympia looked around and realized that even now, with so much already removed, there still wasn't much actual floor to be seen. This was not going to be as easy as she'd hoped.

Okay, she told herself, don't look at the whole mess, just try and take one small section and then another, and then another. It was the same way she approached her sermons. One paragraph or section or topic at a time, and before long she was finished and wondering what in the world she'd been so anxious about before she started.

There was a fairly clearly defined collection of boxes just to the right of the window gap. After five minutes of bending over the first one and feeling her back protesting, she went back into the main house to get one of the kitchen chairs and an oversized trash bag. Now she could sort and dump in one operation ... and five minutes of that had her sneezing nonstop. Back into the main house for a scarf she could tie over her mouth and nose. She was beginning to develop a whole new appreciation for the work that Frederick and Jim had done in her absence. Olympia was determined to do her share. She was like that.

The first box yielded nothing more than a pile of old *National Geographic* magazines. They looked and smelled old, but not old enough to be of any interest or value. She dumped them, box and all, into the trash bag. Then she pulled them back out and flipped through and shook each one. People have been known to slip the most interesting things, such as money, letters and personal documents, into books and magazines. But a half hour of shaking and flapping them yielded nothing than dust and there were still eight more boxes to go. This was going to take a lot longer than she'd originally thought.

Seventeen

When Frederick came home from work he found a straggle-haired Olympia curled in her chair fast asleep. Her face was smudged, and her sweatshirt and work jeans showed the aftereffects of a long dusty day. Next to the still un-emptied trunk he could see an open carton containing vintage copies of *The Saturday Evening Post* magazines. Even Frederick, English as he was and would ever be, knew about *The Saturday Evening Post* and the beloved cover illustrator, Norman Rockwell. There was no doubt in his mind where the carton came from, and he looked forward to hearing all about it when Olympia regained consciousness.

He turned and started to creep back into the kitchen when she awoke.

"Mmph. Oh, hi Frederick. I must have fallen asleep. When did you get in?" She stretched and rubbed her eyes.

"Just now. Let me go wash my hands and get myself a glass of something relaxing, and then you can tell me all about your day."

"Will you call for a pizza while you're up? The take-out menu is right by the phone. Order mushroom, onion and extra cheese for my half, and please ask them to deliver it. They know the way. I know it's an extravagance, but these magazines I found today might just pay for it."

"Crikey," said Frederick.

"Go get yourself a cup of tea or a glass of wine, and I'll tell you what I found. I'd offer to get it for you, but I feel paralyzed from the neck down. I've put in one long day, dearie, but I think I hit a little pay dirt in the process.

"Pay dirt?"

"I think it's a term from the gold rush days."

"Of course, silly me. Being English and all, I should have known, right?"

"Frederick, I'll feel better after you have something to drink in your hand. Go make that happen, please."

When he returned, Olympia had opened both eyes, enjoyed herself a good stretch and was feeling much improved.

She pointed to the box of magazines on the floor. "See that? They are all from the '20s and '30s, and they are in really good condition. A little musty, but otherwise almost pristine."

"Do you think they are they worth anything?"

"I'll go online and look them up after supper. You can find out anything you need to know on the internet these days. It's wonderful."

Frederick wrinkled his nose in mock distain. "I prefer good old book-in-hand research myself, and I probably always will."

"I'm afraid you are a Luddite, my love, morally opposed to change or anything new. Well, it just so happens that I found just the thing for you out there."

"What might that be?" Frederick raised one eyebrow and sipped his tea in the most provocative manner.

"A full set of the *Encyclopedia Britannica* from the 1930s, complete with embossed fake leather binding and all. I checked, and it really is all there. There are even a couple of annual supplements. Worth zero and change, probably."

"You didn't throw it out, did you?" Now both eyebrows were as high up as they could go.

Olympia was about to launch into a diatribe on the evils of hoarding when the pizza delivery lady rang the doorbell. Frederick went to the door, paid the bill and called from the kitchen, "Do you want to use paper plates tonight?"

"Just bring in a roll of paper towels, will you? I'm about to create a whole new category of lazy."

By the time they'd finished the pizza, Olympia had only enough energy to watch TV for a little bit and then crawl into bed. She'd done a full day's work, and she was deservedly and pleasantly tired. Tomorrow she would devote the day to cleaning out the last of the room and making some decisions about what to do next in terms of reconstruction. Her options were walls, the floor, windows and the ceiling—in other words, a complete makeover.

The two spent most of Saturday hauling and dragging the rest of the trash and clutter out into the light of day and chucking most of it into heavy-duty plastic bags, which they took turns holding open. Next to the door there was a small collection of possible treasures piling up in a plastic storage tub. They started with a box of antique medicine bottles. Most were either pale green or light lavender, and many had words and letters stamped into the glass. Frederick added a few books that, whether of value or not, he insisted on keeping. One box, tied with a once white ribbon, brought them both to tears. It was full of baby things, mostly handmade, now brittle with age, full of grit and ragged with moth holes. It was somebody's loving work for a baby born long ago and probably dead long since. Much as she hated to, she heaved the box into the discard bag and reached for the next bundle in the pile.

There was still no key. By mutual agreement they decided to put the trunk and its contents on hold until the cleaning out part was finished. Then Frederick would saw off the lock, and together they would go through it one treasure at a time. Olympia absolutely hated waiting to dive into it, but she suspected that whatever she did find in there could occupy her for hours or more.

On Sunday the outside temperature had gone up to the mid-forties, warm enough to take her van instead of Jim's car. Olympia left early so she could take her time and enjoy the morning. She even cracked open the window and was sure she could smell spring or at least the lovely scent of damp earth under the last of the grey and mud-pitted snow. She also knew it was a false promise. Winter in New England could offer early crocuses one day and a howling blizzard the next. Keeps me from getting complacent, she thought, and signaled for the next exit. A quick check of the time told her she was so early that she would most likely be the one to open the church.

Once she got there she unlocked the door, turned up the heat and went through to her office, where she found Emily's envelope and chocolates sitting on her desk. Without waiting to be asked, she pulled open the box and popped one in her mouth. Never say no to sugar. As she hung her coat behind the door and pulled out her clerical robe, she thought about how to help Emily understand she didn't have to bring her a present every time she came to church.

The sound of voices, footsteps and clattering dishes told her that other people were starting to arrive, and her official Sunday morning had begun. She knew the routine, and she loved it. This was where she belonged and what she did best.

At half past ten, wearing her clerical attire, black doctoral robe and a colorful stole, Olympia walked down the center aisle of the sanctuary and up into the pulpit. There she smiled and held out her arms in welcome and recited the opening prayer. She looked out at the people seated in the pews. Eileen

Sullivan was not among them, but now was not the time to wonder about that. Olympia Brown had work to do.

The service went off without a hitch. There were not as many in attendance as the previous week, but the sermon was well received, the coffee hour was well attended, and the table was well stocked with homemade treats. Even Emily, rather than trying to engage Olympia in conversation, seemed content to say hello, comment on the weather and offer to get her something to eat. Olympia seized the moment and tucked her arm through Emily's.

"Actually, I'm all set right now, but thank you for the chocolates. It was very sweet of you, a nice little surprise when I came in this morning, but you really shouldn't have."

Hurt face. "Why not? Can't I give you a little thank you gift if I want to?"

Olympia tried a different approach. "Of course you can, but I guess I'm trying to say it's not necessary. I like you just the way you are."

"You do?"

"You are a good person and a member of this congregation. Of course I like you."

By half past noon she thought she was home free, or so it seemed. Emily had been duly reassured, and Olympia had managed a short mega-decibel conversation with Forrest Marsh before she was rescued by Catherine Allen. Before she knew it, it was time to go back to her office, collect her things, snag another cookie, and go home. Nope, not quite.

When she stepped into her office, there was another little gift-wrapped surprise on the desk. Of course it was from Emily. This time it was a lavender sachet. Small, non-obligatory, just a token of her appreciation and admiration, said the card.

"Damn," said the Reverend Doctor Olympia Brown. Her first thought was simply to throw it away, but she thought better of it and slipped it into the top drawer of the desk. She liked the scent of lavender. It reminded of her grandmother. She would settle this once and for all the next time Emily came in, but now it was time to head for home.

Sunday afternoon was all about getting the last of the ancient history out of the back room, and when that was finished, a Thai take-out for a celebration dinner. Frederick was delighted with the prospect of a total rehab project. He'd never taken on anything this complicated before, and when she got home he was bursting with ideas, from finding and refinishing old flooring and learning how to plaster walls to installing complex heating and ventilation systems. Olympia was being more cautious in her approach. She had Technicolor memories of some of Frederick's earlier well-intentioned projects. In the end they agreed to apply the KISS principle—Keep It Simple, Stupid!—and to discuss fully each step along the way. In other words, no surprises, Frederick, not even a little one.

When they were full of Pad Thai and green curry, Olympia and Frederick, followed by the cats, once again advanced on the sea chest. Frederick was brandishing his trusty rusty hacksaw, and she was carrying yet another plastic storage tub and an empty trash bag. The scene was set. Frederick began the delicate task of sawing through the clamp on the lock without damaging the surface of the trunk. Olympia helped by holding her breath, and of course, the phone rang.

"Perfect timing," growled Olympia. She struggled to her feet, booted a cat out of the way and ran for the kitchen phone. Frederick was making too much noise in the sitting room for her to hear. They'd waited too long to get to this part, and she was damned if she was going to ask him to stop.

When she returned she announced that it had been Jim on the phone, and he'd landed the adjunct teaching position at ETS. Frederick responded by holding up the separated lock. He'd graciously waited until she returned so they could lift off the cover together.

Olympia didn't know what she was expecting to find, and she had to keep reminding herself to breathe. Slowly, bit by bit, box by parcel by bundled and string-tied sheaves of papers, including the mysterious black metal box, they methodically emptied the chest. The cats had perched themselves side by side on the coffee table and watched every move, but even they began to sneeze.

"I didn't know history was going to be so dusty," said Frederick, wiping his eyes.

"It's going to take longer than I thought to go through it all. Oh, my God, will you look at this?"

She grabbed Frederick's arm with her free hand. In the other was the metal box she'd just extracted from the trunk.

"What is it?"

"It's an old locket. Look, you can open it. It has two tiny photographs in it. It's got to be Leanna and little Jared."

Olympia couldn't explain why she was crying, but then, she didn't need to. Of course Frederick understood. Finally, here she was, literally in the palm of her hand, the woman whose house she lived in, whose words she'd been reading and savoring, and who, like herself, struggled to make her own way.

"I wonder whatever happened to the little boy?" asked Frederick.

"I've often asked that question myself. If he was born in the early 1860s, he could have lived well into the 1940s. Miss

Winslow died in 1926. I looked it up in the town records one day when I was happened to be in town hall. I couldn't find anything there about him."

"Well, if she told everyone he was adopted or that she'd taken him in, there might not be any official papers."

"I wonder if I can get hold of some old school records. I might be able to find something there. Maybe we should give that some thought. I would so like to know."

Olympia was pressing the locket against her heart with both hands.

"One mystery at a time, my love," said Frederick with a fond smile. "This trunk is going to keep us busy and sneezing for weeks, if not months, to come."

"You know, I think I've had all the excitement I can stand for one day. I'm absolutely exhausted. Eileen Sullivan is coming in again tomorrow, and I need to be fully present when she does."

"Well, if anyone can help her, you can."

"It's not about helping. It's about listening, and if that's helping, so be it. I don't envy her, but I do understand. I guess that's why I'm so committed to being there for her. You know, been there, done that."

Olympia smiled a wistful smile and tucked the little locket inside the diary, where it would not be a temptation for the cats. Now she was ready for bed.

"Say, what about that other one, the clinger, the one who hangs on your every word? Was she in church today?" asked Frederick.

Olympia nodded. "I'd almost forgotten about her. Yes, she was there, and she was okay, I think. She did leave me a little box of chocolates and later on a lavender sachet, but when I think about it, they're pretty harmless."

"If it makes her happy, what's the problem?"

"In and of itself nothing, I suppose, but it's as if she's always trying to please me or get my attention. I'm the minister. She doesn't have to buy my affection or my caring, and yet I could never say that to her."

"So what did you say?"

"I gave her a little hug and thanked her. I'm seeing her on Wednesday. I'll surely come up with something by then."

Eighteen

When Olympia arrived at the church on Monday morning, Charlotte told her she had two messages, one from Eileen Sullivan confirming her appointment at eleven and the other from Emily, who left a number and asked if Olympia wasn't too busy, could she give please her a call before noon.

Olympia looked perplexed. "I wonder what that's about."

"Are you talking to me?" said Charlotte.

Olympia shook her head. "I guess I was thinking out loud. I probably shouldn't ask this, but I'm going to anyway. In professional confidence, what can you tell me about Emily Goodale? We both know the church administrator is the one who really knows the ins and outs of a place, and I won't tell if you won't."

Charlotte shook her head and began rolling a pencil back and forth in her fingers.

"She's sort of a lost soul, isn't she? I don't know a whole lot about her. I do know she grew up here on the Cape, over in Falmouth, I think, and she works at The Crepe Codder. It's a year-round restaurant in Mashpee. I know, because she's waited on me a couple of times. It's a great restaurant. You should go sometime; she'd probably love to see you."

I'm not so sure about that, thought Olympia, as Charlotte continued with her story.

"I think she lives somewhere between here and there. All we have in the church directory is a PO number in Sandwich."

"Wow, you can keep all that address stuff in your head. There are days I can't remember my own phone number."

"I do the mailings, remember, and she sticks out because she's changed her mailing address twice since she started coming here. Now that I think about it, if she keeps changing her address, she probably really is a lost soul."

"Hmm."

Olympia was deliberately keeping her face in neutral, but inside her brain the obvious questions were hop-scotching all over themselves. Why had Emily lied about where she grew up and what she did for work? Or had she told Olympia the truth and told a different story to Charlotte when she signed the membership book?

"Like I said, she's an odd little duck. Kind of high-maintenance, if you ask me, which you didn't. She does glom on to people, but by now it looks as if you know that already."

"Let's just say I'm getting a clearer understanding of said little duck. Thanks, Charlotte. I'll give her a call and see what she wants."

What Olympia learned when she called Emily was that she simply wanted to confirm her Wednesday meeting and ask if she could take Olympia to lunch afterward. Olympia rolled her eyes in the privacy of her office and said thank you, but she wasn't sure if that was going to be possible, and could she let Emily know on Wednesday?

The rest of her morning was a random collection of phone calls, reviewing meeting minutes, checking the pastoral care and visit list and, when she looked up from her computer, a surprise visit from Forrest Marsh. She could see Charlotte Loring standing in the doorway directly behind him, grinning like the proverbial Cheshire Cat.

"I told Forrest you have a conference call in fifteen minutes," yelled Charlotte. She was pointing to her right eye and winking madly. "Will you want to take it?"

Olympia had to look away to keep from laughing. "Thank you, Charlotte, I probably should. These are so difficult to set up, you know."

She stood and extended her hand. "Well, hello, Forrest, what a nice surprise. I will have to take that phone call, but we have a few minutes. Come in and sit down, and tell me what you'd like to talk about."

"Huh?"

"Have a seat! Would you like a chocolate?" she hollered.

In Brookfield Frederick was preparing for a trip to the local dump. He'd dragged the last of the items to be discarded outside and loaded them onto the back of his own vintage vehicle, a 1950 bright yellow Ford pickup. After that he went back into the house and returned with an armful of bungee cords that were wiggling and bouncing like demented caterpillars. Frederick, wise and considerate man that he was, would not have his trash flying all over the streets of Brookfield. Methodically he tugged and snapped and bunched his colorful load into a well constricted and manageable heap. He stood back and admired his handiwork for a few well deserved moments and then dusted off his hands and hopped into the cab. Frederick had a driving routine. First he buckled up, then he turned on the radio, then he checked the rear and side mirrors. When all was done in the proper fashion, he wiggled the steering wheel, turned the key and set off.

He liked going to the dump, as one never knew what one might find there. For him it was hunting without a gun. He'd come to know some of the regulars there and looked forward to catching up on the latest town gossip. This called for a cup of take-out coffee. A gentleman, particularly an English gentleman, would never consider going to the dump unfortified.

By now he knew the lady in the take-out window at the local drive-through. She recognized his accent and knew that before eleven, Frederick drank tea, but between eleven and noon, he drank coffee. If nothing else, and there was a whole lot of else, Frederick was a creature of habit. So when he pulled up to the window, Betty was smiling and holding out a tall milky coffee, no sugar, with his name on it.

"So where're ya going today, Mr. Watkins?"

He gestured at the rear of the truck with his free hand. "I'm taking this motley collection to the local dump, there to cast it into oblivion for all eternity."

"What collection? I don't see anything. Maybe you, like, forgot to load the stuff. I've done that."

"But …" Frederick twisted around in his seat and looked deeply into a vast and empty truck bed.

"Oh, bother," said the English gentleman. "I'm sure I loaded it, but it appears I might have forgotten to secure the tailgate."

While Frederick was trying to come to terms with the mystery of the missing trash, Olympia was recovering her voice from yelling at the irascible and entertaining Mr. Marsh. The object of his visit had been to tell her more about the history of the church and its founding families. She found it all wonderfully interesting, but even fifteen minutes with him left her hoarse, and she was more than grateful when Charlotte interrupted to remind her she had a phone call to make.

"Thanks for the rescue," croaked Olympia after he'd left.

"No problem. I had the same arrangement with Reverend Phil. Forrest is a grand old man, and we all love him dearly, but he can go on."

Olympia nodded in silent agreement. She then pointed to her mouth, patted her stomach and pantomimed turning car keys and wiggling a steering wheel.

"Going to lunch?"

Affirmative nod.

"I'll be gone when you come back, so make sure you take your key.

A second affirmative nod.

In the interest of saving time, Olympia went off to the nearest place she could find and ordered a take-out salad and a double cappuccino. This way she could enjoy a quiet lunch and a few minutes listening to WFCC Classical 107.5 Cape Cod alone in her office before meeting with Eileen. Alas, her pleasant anticipation dissolved when she returned to find a vanilla-scented votive candle in a heart-shaped crystal dish. She could smell it the second she stepped over the threshold. Olympia hated scented candles. Strong perfumes of any gender or persuasion made her wheeze, and the scented gifts from Emily Goodale were beginning to make her gag. Furthermore, when had she left it? It must have been before Charlotte left for the day. Olympia frowned in consternation.

Cold as it was, she heaved open a window and took the candle out into the parish hall and set it on one of the tables where she could no longer smell it. When she returned, her office was freezing, but at least it didn't smell like vanilla ice cream. Now she would shut the windows, eat her lunch and think of something tactful and firm that would put an end to Miss Goodale's seemingly unstoppable largesse once and for all. She yanked the windows back down with more force than was really necessary, but it felt good when she did it.

By the time Eileen arrived, Olympia had calmed down and was really looking forward to seeing her. She declined Olympia's offer of tea and or hot chocolate, saying she'd just had lunch and was still being careful about what and when she ate.

"I find that several small meals rather than three big ones seem to work right now. When I get hungry, which seems to be all the time, I find if I eat a little bit and then have a little more later on, I don't get so nauseated." Eileen tossed her coat and scarf over the back of the chair and sat down.

Olympia smiled, remembering her own pregnancies and thinking there hadn't been a cupboard or a refrigerator big enough to accommodate her appetite.

"The nausea usually stops after the first three months. After that you're running to the bathroom all the time. If it isn't one thing, it's another. Other than that, how are you feeling?"

"Tired, stressed, and at the same time ..." She paused and pursed her lips in thought. "I don't know how to say it, but I feel better in my heart."

"Why do you think that might be?"

Eileen folded her hands together and stared down into her lap before answering. "I've decided I'm going to keep the baby. I'm not poor, my parents will help, and after that, what will be, will be. Now that she's over the shock of hearing it, my mother's starting to get excited at the prospect of being a grandmother again. I'll be living at home, so she'll get all the hands-on baby time she wants."

"What about your father?"

"He's coming around, but I think he'll be a pain."

"How so."

"He's a doctor. He thinks he knows everything there is to know. Well, he probably does, but he's my father, so he's not going to be my doctor."

"Have you chosen a doctor yet?"

Eileen shook her head. "I will ask him to recommend one. He'll like that."

On the inside Olympia was fairly bursting with happiness, but she was careful to keep her mounting ebullience under control.

"There's so much to think about. I suppose there would be whichever decision I came to, but it all feels pretty overwhelming."

"Whatever the circumstances, Eileen, bringing a child into the world is a huge step, and it will change your life forever. But people have been bringing children into the world ever since there were people, and somehow we manage. You will, too."

Eileen bit her lip and began twisting her fingers again.

"Do you want to tell me what you're thinking about?" asked Olympia.

"I've been thinking a lot about the baby's father. His name is Jimmy Bakewell. He's really nice."

"And?"

"Well, it didn't take long for my parents to figure out who he was. He's the only guy I've been seeing for the last year. My mother's pushing me to tell him and get married ASAP, but I said no. I like him well enough, but I don't want to get married right now. I'm not at all sure he's the one I want to spend the rest of my life with, but I do have to tell him. It's his baby, too. Besides, in a couple of months it's going to be obvious, and it wouldn't be fair to say nothing and let him find out that way."

"I think you've made a wise decision," said Olympia.

"I don't know how wise it is, but it's the one I and my parents are going to have to live with." Another pause. "I really appreciate your listening to all of this and not trying to make up my mind for me. Thank you, Reverend, you've been awesome."

"I'm not going anywhere, Eileen. I live in Brookfield, about twenty minutes across the Bridge. "I'll be here at Salt Rock for another nine weeks, so you know you can call if you need to."

"I think I'll be okay now. I really do."

"I think you will, too, but do keep in touch if you want to. I care about that baby, too. You will tell me, won't you?"

Eileen nodded. "I called Jimmy before I came up here and asked him if we could go out for a drive later this afternoon. I have no idea how he's going to take it."

"There's no telling, so I might suggest you be prepared for anything. Remember how confused and upset you were when you first learned of it. You've had a couple of weeks to come to terms with it. If he's just finding out, he'll need some time, same as you did."

"I'm meeting him in an hour, so I'd better get going."

Both women stood, and Olympia held out her arms. Eileen melted into the hug and held on for dear life, hers and the life she was carrying. "Thank you, thank you, thank you," she said into Olympia's shoulder.

"I'll pray for you all, Eileen. Take good care, and keep both of yourselves warm. It's freezing out there."

After she left, Olympia collected her own things and made ready to do the same. As she walked around the parish hall to check the heat and the several doors that led to the outside, she could she hear the faint sound of organ music coming from the sanctuary. Must be the organist practicing, she thought. I'll stick my head in the door and say hi. But when she did, the church was cold and dark and empty. That's strange, she thought. I know I heard music, and I know it was coming from here.

Her first thought was to go exploring in the organ loft to see if someone had left the speaker system on and something was coming through it. No, she argued with herself, whatever it is or was, it has stopped, and I'm dead on my feet. I need to go home right now.

After dinner that evening Frederick led his wife out into the almost office, as they were now calling it, there to show her how much he'd accomplished that day. He stood in the doorway and pointed with pride. The entire floor was now visible. All the trash, junk and miscellaneous leftovers from a bygone era were gone. While it could not yet be called a thing of beauty, it was a lovely open space fairly bursting with potential. At least that's how they both saw it, sort of.

She saw a workspace, a desk, a pull-out sofa for guests or grandchildren, a picture window, a small oriental on the floor and plants and more plants. He saw floor boards, skirting boards, wall board and window fittings, and all that lovely carpentry equipment he would be forced to acquire, all in the service of creating an office for his lady wife, of course.

"So what did you do with all the junk?" she asked.

"Funny you should ask," said Frederick.

Nineteen

Olympia was not surprised to find Emily Goodale sitting in the outer office when she arrived on Wednesday morning.

"Oh gosh, am I late?" Olympia pulled back her sleeve and looked at her watch.

"Oh, no, Reverend, I'm usually early. I don't like to keep people waiting. I think that's rude."

Behind her Charlotte rolled her eyes and stared up at the ceiling.

"Just give me a minute to run to the bathroom, will you? Too much coffee on the way here."

Emily looked crestfallen. "Oh, you won't want any more then, will you? I went and bought some for you."

"No problem, I just have to make room for it. I never met a cup of coffee I didn't like. I'll be right back."

The joke was lost on Emily.

When the two were settled in Olympia's office, each with their fresh containers of coffee close to hand, Olympia opened the conversation.

"I didn't get a chance to thank you for the chocolates you left me. The coffee hour on Sunday was an absolute madhouse. It was great, though. Who can complain about happy, chatty people on a Sunday morning? It's a minister's fondest dream and greatest wish all rolled up into one. So thank you, they were delicious, and they are all gone. I gave the last one to Forrest Marsh."

Emily smiled. "You should know that people are talking about what a good speaker you are. Word gets around the

Cape pretty fast. That means more people on a Sunday morning."

"Thank you for the kind words, Emily, but I think it was more likely a combination of good weather and no place else to go, plus the quality of the goodies at coffee hour. Did you make some of those?"

Emily looked down into her lap and smiled. "I made the hermits. I hope you got one. They went pretty fast."

"So it's you I have to thank. They were unbelievable. I wrapped one up and planned to bring it home for later, but I didn't even make it to the bridge before I attacked it. What's your secret?"

"I always use a little more molasses and ginger than the recipe calls for, and I make them with strong coffee rather than milk or water. The other thing I do is use light raisins instead of the dark ones. I think it makes a difference." Emily was beaming now. She was almost pretty when she smiled. Olympia found it a welcome change from the perpetual worried half-frown that seemed to be Emily's signature expression.

"You seem to be in good spirits. I'm happy to see that. Is there anything specific you'd like to talk about today?"

Emily slumped down in her chair, and her face went from pleased and proud to the familiar anxious fret. "I suppose I shouldn't even say this, but I'm already feeling bad about your leaving in April. You're only going to be here for another nine weeks. I counted. You don't know what it means to have someone I trust that wants to talk to me."

Olympia spoke gently. "Emily, everyone knows I'm only here for the three months Reverend Rutledge is on sabbatical. Of course I want to do a good job of tending his flock in his absence, but all I'm really doing is keeping the seat warm. I've made a ministry of short ministries, interims, short chaplaincies and filling in for sabbaticals. It's interesting and varied work, and it suits me to a T."

"Does that mean you want to leave already?" Now she looked downright horrified.

Olympia smiled and shook her head. "Hardly, Emily. I don't live far from here, and there's every good chance that we'll meet again after my contract is completed. When I'm not working at a specific church, I often come down to the Cape as a workshop leader or guest preacher. So don't worry, I'm a dyed-in-the-wool New Englander, and I'm not going anywhere."

Emily appeared to be marginally comforted but soon began to fidget. "I'm sorry, I didn't mean to sound so clingy, but I'm sure you can understand that with my foster care background, I have a lot of issues around trust and attachment. You are really helping me with that."

I'm not so sure about that, thought Olympia, but now is not the time to bring it up. "I'm pleased to hear you say that."

"So I can come back again next week?"

Take out the kid gloves, and proceed with caution, Olympia. "To be honest, I think it would good to wait a week and use that time to think about what we talk about today."

"But …"

"You'll have to trust me on this, Emily. Thinking time is every bit as important as actual talking time, maybe even more so. But this coming Saturday I'm going to be working on a project with the youth group, and if you're free, I could use some help setting up and then just being an extra set of hands in the kitchen. It will be a bit messy, but it will be fun. They want to have a Valentine's Day bake sale, and I said I'd help them cook. From what I learned about those hermits you made, I think you are just the person for the job. What do you think?"

Olympia watched as Emily shape-shifted once again from anxious to ebullient in under three seconds.

"Really, you want me to help you? Oh, that's wonderful. Let me check my schedule. I might have to swap shifts with someone, but I'd love to do it. I'll let you know by the end of tomorrow."

"Gee, I thought since you work the night shift, it shouldn't interfere with anything, or has that changed?"

Emily never missed a beat. "Sometimes I work an earlier shift if someone needs me to. I think it's important to help out when you can. You never know when you'll need a favor in return."

"I couldn't agree more, and while we're on the subject of work, why don't you tell me more about the people you work with? Do you have any special friends there? You said you work at a nursing home, right?"

"They call it an extended care facility. We have a little of everything—Alzheimer's, rehab, respite care, even some hospice patients. I don't work with them, though. I get too attached."

"I can understand that. Hospice work isn't for everyone."

"Tell me about the youth group, will you? How many of them will be there? Should I bring something?"

Olympia knew when a subject had been deliberately changed, and she wasn't going to push back, at least not right now. She also knew the time would come when she would have no choice.

"Just bring yourself and an apron. As I said, the kids are guaranteed to be messy, and you might as well be prepared. Part of the project is to decide what we want to make and then go shopping for the ingredients. Now that I think of it, I might need you as an extra driver. My van will hold six, and if you can take four, we have it covered. That way, I won't need to bother one of the parents, and at that age, kids do not want their parents in attendance for anything."

By now Emily was positively glowing. To all appearances Olympia had succeeded in finding a way for her to be genuinely useful in the church community. At the same time she would have a chance to observe this woman in action without it being obvious. Double mission semi-accomplished, she thought. It's all about feeling needed, and sometimes the best of us need a little help in that department. It's also about getting a closer look at this person and by doing so, maybe understanding a little more about what's going on beneath the surface.

Olympia checked the time as unobtrusively as she could with a quick glance at the digital clock on her desk. She wanted to say something about the gift giving but decided the opportunity had passed. Setting firm time limits on Emily's visits was more important. No doubt there would be another opportunity to discuss the gifts.

After Emily left Olympia walked into Charlotte's office and asked if she had a few minutes.

"Sure, what's up?" said Charlotte.

"Well a couple of things. First of all, was the church organist practicing in here on Monday afternoon?"

"Not that I know of. She usually practices on Thursday. I love listening to it. She's really good; we're lucky to have her. Why do you ask?"

"I thought I heard organ music when I was getting ready to go home on Monday. I must be hearing things.'

"Well, it sounds like you've just been accepted," said Charlotte.

Olympia looked perplexed. "What are you talking about?"

"That would be our dear departed, but ever present, Jeremy Adams, the church ghost. Only people he likes can ever hear him play. He must like you."

Anyone else hearing this would have laughed out loud or dismissed it as pure fantasy, but Olympia accepted it as gospel truth.

"I have another question."

"Mmmm?"

"On Monday I went out to get myself some lunch while you were still here. Remember? Before you left, did Emily Goodale come in here and leave something in my office?"

"Not that I know of. Why, did you find something?"

Olympia nodded. "A scented candle. Strong scents can make me wheeze, so I put it out in the parish hall where I couldn't smell it. You want it?"

"No, thanks, its fine where it is, but I did wonder where it came from. Are you sure it was from her?"

"No question, but I want to know when she did it."

"Well, I did go to the bathroom before I left. Maybe she scooted in then, and I never saw her."

"Possibly," said Olympia, "but if not then, when?" Olympia didn't add that what she really wanted to know is how Emily got into the office. These were troubling thoughts and more ill-fitting pieces to a curious puzzle that was not coming together.

"Oh, and one more thing, Charlotte. Is the youth group Valentine bake on the calendar for Saturday afternoon?"

"It is indeed. You'll have a blast with those kids. They're great."

"All kids are great if you give them half a chance."

"Preach on, sister," said Charlotte.

The rest of the week was a typical round of pastoral calls and visits, sermon preparation and meetings. In other words, for a minister it was blessedly uneventful. There were no pastoral crises, nobody skidding into the office with their hair on fire over a misplaced comma, and no whining e-mails from aggrieved parishioners.

Things were relatively quiet on the home front, as well. Olympia and Frederick had not crossed swords over the plans for the almost-office because each of their plans was personality specific: colors and furnishings versus tools and construction. No problem, that is, until Frederick decided what he really needed was to build a workshop first so he would not have to do the preparation carpentry in the same space he was renovating.

After an evening of impassioned illogic, both agreed that one space at a time under construction was all that the marriage or the house could withstand. A solemn promise that the very next project would indeed be a workshop for Frederick settled the matter for the time being … maybe.

Twenty

By noon on Saturday Olympia's sermon was finished, the hymns and readings already chosen, and her Sunday outfit was freed of cat hair and hanging on the closet door. Olympia was ready to rock and roll with the SRYF, as the Salt Rock Youth Fellowship called themselves. She was also ready to spend some quality time with Emily Goodale in a new and different setting. Here they would be equals working side by side, up to their elbows in flour and sugar and surrounded by wonderful, energetic kids. Emily would have a chance to shine on her own with Olympia and ten noisy teenagers to cheer her on. By all indications, this is what she needed more than anything else, to belong and be valued for who she was.

They were all scheduled to meet at two, go shopping for ingredients and start cooking about three. She figured they'd be done by six and told the parents to come by then to pick up their offspring and score some free samples.

Olympia noted with some pleasure that Emily seemed to have taken a bit more care with her appearance today. She was wearing freshly ironed jeans, a pink smiley face tee-shirt and sparkly earrings. But it wasn't just the clothes. Emily was actually wearing a touch of lipstick and a hint of eye shadow and, Olympia was certain, a splash of flowery perfume. Good for her, she thought. Care and attention to appearance is healthy and normal.

Let the chaos begin. The merry, flour-dusted, music-blaring madness that ensued would never have been described in any seminary textbook, but Olympia was ready for it. She'd spent more than one afternoon cooking with her sons when they were in their teens. She was not dismayed when Phillip Wainwright cracked an egg on his sister Annie's head or when Alibell had a meltdown when she burned the chocolate. It's all part of the process, she told herself, and in the middle of it all, close beside her, Emily was buzzing right along. She was mixing, testing, rolling out cookies, washing up the utensils and licking spoons. Other than sticking a little too close to Olympia, which was surely understandable with all those kids flying around, she was doing just fine. Olympia found herself smiling warm approval in Emily's direction and offering words of encouragement and appreciation whenever she could. Emily was pink-cheeked and smiling and obviously comfortable with the kids as they careened around the kitchen. Olympia allowed herself the teensiest breath of relief.

In the days to come she would recall how well they had worked together, and then she would ask herself what she had missed. But for now, all lights were green, and it was full speed ahead.

At the end of the afternoon, they had a table full of baked goods: a sinful variety of cookies, Emily's heavenly hermits, Olympia's deadly fudge, and seven—count them, seven— devil's food cakes, food fit for a decadent king, the heavenly host and a bunch of voracious Unitarians. She was as proud of them all as she could be. The kids were earning money for a ski trip, and with her encouragement they had offered to give half their earnings to the local food pantry.

What they didn't know was that Olympia had quietly solicited some matching funds from a few people in the congregation. The result was that at the end of the day, the kids would end up with all of their earnings and still be able make a donation to help people in need. Talk about win-win.

Olympia was feeling pretty damned good about herself and rightfully so.

After the last teenager bounced out the door, Olympia and Emily, both looking a little worse for wear, set about wiping down the counters and the stovetop one last time. The kitchen had to be in pristine condition for Sunday morning, or there would be hell to pay. They didn't teach that in seminary either, but Olympia was a fast learner.

When they well and truly finished, Olympia untied her apron and slipped it over her head. As she did so, Emily moved in close behind her and kissed her on the back of the neck. Olympia flinched, gasped and whirled around in one stunned moment.

"Wha …?"

"I'm sorry, Olympia, I didn't mean to scare you. I just couldn't help myself." To Olympia's wide-eyed stare she added softly, "Don't tell me you're surprised. Why else would you ask me to come and help you? I know how you feel about me. "

Olympia took an involuntary step backward, but Emily caught her by the hand and held on. Her voice was low and intense.

"Before I met you I could never have imagined myself falling in love with a woman, but I've been attracted to you since the day I called you on the telephone back in December. I think it started with the sound of your voice. You have a beautiful speaking voice, you know, and even more than that, you seemed happy to hear from me. And now look, here we are." Emily was smiling, but the muscles along the side of her neck were tight.

"Emily, let go of my hand, take off your apron and come into my office. I'm afraid you've gotten mixed messages, and we need to sort this out right now."

"No, Reverend, I think it's you who doesn't understand, but I'm happy to come and talk. You see, it's all new to me, too, and from what I'm told, these things take time."

Once they were seated well apart from each other, Olympia didn't waste any time getting straight to the matter at hand. The smile was gone from Emily's face now, and in its place was the intense, wary look of a hunter. Olympia was both the hunted and the warden. She could not and would not let this go any further. She had to proceed with the utmost sensitivity, kindness and compassion. This was the stuff of a minister's worst nightmare, only it was real, and she was right in the middle of it. Tread gently and carefully, she told herself. A misstep or wrong move here could make things even worse than they already are.

Olympia spoke carefully, putting every ounce of her training, her experience and her calling into her words.

"Emily, when a person is hurt and lonely, it can be easy to attach more meaning to a gesture of kindness and friendship than is actually intended by the person reaching out to you. I'm afraid this might have happened with you."

Emily, now solemn faced, looked directly at Olympia. "You can't tell me you didn't know what was going on. Why do you think I left you all those little gifts? They were my way of saying thank you for being so nice to me. I was letting you know that I understood what you were trying to tell me without actually saying it. I know a minister can't appear to pay special attention to any one person. That's why I kept them small. They were love notes wrapped up in paper and string, but I was careful when I left them so nobody would see me. Don't you see? I was protecting you from any kind of gossip."

It took a herculean effort on Olympia's part not to look shocked or horrified. She felt as if she was swimming against a very strange and relentless tide, a tide that would not turn back but would only keep advancing until it consumed everything in its path. She tried again. This time her voice was stronger, her words more deliberate.

"Emily. I remember you telling me you had a very troubled childhood."

"At least you got that part right." Emily swallowed and licked her lips.

"This isn't a contest, Emily. I'm trying to bring us to a place of understanding, and the last thing I want to do is hurt you in the process. You need to know that even if you are having strong feelings for me, they are not being reciprocated. I care for you as a parishioner and as a good and decent woman and as a sister human being, but I am not, nor will I ever be, in love with you."

"But you accepted the gifts, and you asked me to come and help today. If you didn't love me, why would you do that?" Emily was flushed now and obviously fighting back tears.

"I'm afraid you've misinterpreted my pastoral concern for your spiritual and emotional welfare. I am not in love with you, Emily. You need to understand and accept that reality. Once you do, we can both put this behind us and find a way for you to be comfortable here as part of the whole congregation. Churches are made up of people who come together to build spiritual and religious community and support one another in the joys and challenges which are part of our individual lives. You need to find a way to be part of the whole community rather than dependent on a single person. My job as a minister is to try and make that happen."

Emily was openly weeping now, and in any other circumstance, Olympia would have reached for her hand or opened her arms to hug her. It would have been the worst thing she could have done, and she knew it. She also needed to bring this meeting to an end. Olympia held out the box of tissues she kept on the corner of her desk.

It was a few minutes before Emily was able to speak. "I suppose you want me to leave the church."

"The idea never occurred to me, and I don't consider it part of our discussion. I do want you to think about what I've just been saying to you and know that your feelings, while human, are misdirected. They are not and will never be reciprocated. I'm still your minister, and I want find a way for you to have a happy and healthy place in this congregation."

"Do you really think that's possible now?"

The tone of the conversation had shifted.

"I think almost anything can be possible if we want it to be, and then we both work to make it happen."

"Whatever."

"I want you to think on what I said to you, and then I'd like us to have another conversation early next week. Can you do that?"

"If you say so." Emily's mouth was a flat angry line that cut through the middle of her face.

"Why don't you come into my office after the service tomorrow, and we'll pick a day and a time? Will that work for you?"

"Look, I gotta go. It's late. I have stuff to do." She was wiggling her foot and making a great show of looking at her watch.

"Of course, Emily, but I would like you to come and see me tomorrow. This conversation needs to have a compassionate closure."

"Right." Red faced with either shame or anger, Emily collected her things and left without a word.

Olympia waited until she heard the main door click shut, and then she stood and watched through the window as Emily drove off. The woman's anger was understandable and, when she thought about it, probably a healthy reaction to what had just happened. Olympia had no idea how this would eventually play out. There were any number of directions it could take. She knew one thing for sure and that was not to try to handle this by herself.

As much as she didn't want to bother Phil Rutledge while he was on sabbatical, she knew he needed to be in on this, and she needed his advice ASAP. His home and his cell numbers were both in the well-thumbed church directory next to the phone. After she called him, she would write a full report documenting everything that had just happened and send a copy to her District Supervisor. Then, when she got home, she'd tell Frederick and call Jim.

She reached for the phone and dialed the unfamiliar number, hoping against hope Phil Rutledge would be home.

Outside in the dark, Emily was back. As she approached the church, she switched off her headlights, turned into the parking lot and wheeled the car silently around to her hiding spot behind the building. She could see by the lights in her office that Olympia was still there. Emily got out of the car, crept up to the window and stood watching Olympia talking on the phone and wondered who she might be talking to.

"Oh, I'll come back, all right, Reverend," she hissed into the freezing night air, "only it won't be tomorrow. It will be when you least expect it, and when I do, you won't even know I'm there until I decide it's time."

Emily's heart didn't break that easily, and she knew that if Olympia was any kind of a minister, she'd have figured it out by now.

Twenty-One

When Olympia got home that night, she felt like a deflated balloon. Earlier in the day she'd been puffed full of enthusiasm and good will. Now, seven hours later, she felt wilted and drained as though she was sagging in all directions. Frederick took one look at her as she came in through the kitchen door and went straight for the telephone.

"Pizza, Thai, or Mexican?"

"Wine, a hot shower and then Mexican, please. Anything vegetarian, I'm too tired to choose, much less think."

Fredrick made an executive decision and poured her a glass of wine. Then he pulled off her coat and held out one of the kitchen chairs.

"Was it that bad? How many kids? Anything left of the church kitchen?"

"The kids were great, every last one of them. It was Emily Goodale. She seems to have fallen in love with me."

"Smart woman," quipped Frederick.

Olympia responded with a frostbitten glare. "I'm not joking."

"I'm sorry, love, is she the one who's been tagging after you?"

Olympia nodded. "I really thought I had it all in hand. You know, find her something to do, make her feel valuable, include her, and I got it a hundred and eighty degrees wrong."

"People hear what they want to hear, not always what you intend for them to hear."

Olympia threw back her head and groaned in response.

"Tell you what. I'm going upstairs and fill the tub. You top up your wine and have a good long soak for yourself, very therapeutic. I'll phone for supper and call you when it arrives. Then you can give me all the lurid details over a vegetarian enchilada and some refried beans."

"Maybe just the enchilada. Beans could be counteractive to a serious discussion."

"Whatever do you mean, my darling?" With his eyebrows raised and his mouth in the false prim position, Frederick was the picture of wide-eyed innocence.

"What I mean is, it might be hard to make myself heard over your farting."

Frederick looked injured, but then he grinned. "Whatever it takes to ease the tension in your body and put a smile on your face, my love, and if refried beans is the secret ingredient to getting a smile out of you, then I say bring them on."

"Maybe if we both have some," said Olympia with a tired smile. Only Frederick could make a conversation about farts and beans sound like a Shakespearean love sonnet. The man was a wonder.

An hour later, when she was a new woman, Frederick again asked about her day. "So you say you called the resident minister. I'm pleased to hear that. What did he have to say?"

Wearing her robe and slippers, Olympia was curled up in her chair with a cat in her lap and a cup of chamomile tea in her hands. Frederick, having just topped up the fire in the woodstove, was nursing a "toothful" of Jim's lovely brandy. He was sprawled on the sofa with his feet on the coffee table.

"I called Phil Rutledge the minute Emily left. I really didn't want to bother him, but he assured me it was the right thing to do. He knows all about her, but now that I think about it, I'm not so sure he does."

"What on earth is that supposed to mean?"

"When I asked him what he knew of her background, he gave me a totally different story from what Emily told me. And what Emily told me is totally different from what Charlotte, the church administrator told me. That's three and counting."

"Which one do you think is the real one?"

"Damned if I know. I'm beginning to think this woman is not just anxious and needy."

"Then what exactly is she?" asked Frederick.

Olympia rubbed her chin. "I don't know for sure, but she might be a bit, or even a lot more, troubled than I originally thought."

"What else did the other minister have to say?

"Well, for openers she told him she was a former nun and had finally left the convent after fifteen years of discontent and misery. One day she walked into Salt Rock and hung on like a barnacle. At first she was all gung ho, couldn't do enough for him and the church. Then one day, blam, she's cold and distant with no explanation."

"What happened after that?"

"Phil said it was lots of dark looks and darker mutterings. He hoped that with him on sabbatical and out of sight for a while, she'd calm down."

"Sounds as if she's simply adjusted her sights, and now you're the one in the crosshairs."

"Not a very comforting image," said Olympia.

"I think you need to be on guard."

"And I think you are right."

Frederick blinked several times. "Do my eyes and ears deceive me? Did I just hear you agree with me on the subject of your personal safety?"

"Unfortunately, you did." Olympia was scratching Cadeau under the chin, and the cat was purring in ecstatic response.

"So what are you going to do about it?"

"I followed the professional guidelines to the letter. I spoke to her directly. I called the settled minister and told him. I wrote a detailed description of the incident, dated it and sent it to my District Supervisor, and now I've just told you. Tomorrow, I'll tell one or two members of the board. There's nothing else I can do right now except never to be alone with her and weigh and measure every word I say to her. Even then, who knows what she'll say or do? I've never dealt with anything like this before."

"Do you think she could be a threat to you personally?"

Olympia frowned, shook her head and continued rubbing and scratching the cat before responding.

"I don't know, Frederick, I really don't know."

"Be careful, darling."

On Sunday morning Emily Goodale was absent and unaccounted for, and Olympia was distinctly uneasy because of it. She felt that she'd have some measure of control of the situation if Emily were there; but in this case, out of sight was definitely not out of mind. What might the woman be thinking, or worse, thinking about doing? She was an unknown quantity and a loose cannon muddled up into one untidy mess. And what about all her different stories? That was something else Olympia needed to check into.

There was, however, no time to dwell on this. The youth group was having their bake sale, and they were almost as hyper as they had been the night before. By noontime every last crumb had either been sold or licked off a finger, and the triumphant teens were almost four hundred dollars richer than they had been the previous evening. Olympia decided to wait to tell them about the matching funds until the following Sunday, when all the figures would be in and the accounting complete. They were too excited to hear anything just now, and it was good fun just seeing them there, being raucous and boisterous and crashing into each other like half-grown puppies.

Meanwhile, she wanted to catch Catherine Allen before she left and give her a brief accounting of the uncomfortable events of the night before. Alas, she was nowhere to be found, so Olympia made a mental note to self to call her the minute she got home. Something of this nature can never be put on the back burner, because left unattended it will simmer, then smolder and eventually burst into flame. Olympia shivered at the image of her own uncomfortable metaphor and made ready to go home.

In Brookfield Frederick was tending the home fires and serving as both home secretary and telephone monitor. That morning all of Olympia's children, including her two sons, Randall and Malcolm, and her daughter Laura, called in to say hello and asked to have their mother call them back. Then, no sooner had Frederick settled back into his most immediate project, framing out the windows (and freezing in the abundance of fresh air blowing in through the hole in the wall) when the phone rang again. This time no one was there, and Frederick was none too happy about the interruption. He realized it was the third or the fourth time in recent memory this had happened. Maybe he should mention this to Olympia.

The next time the phone rang Frederick refused to stop what he was doing and let the answering machine get it. When he listened to the message later, he heard their friend Jim, saying he needed to come get the car for a couple of days, and was Wednesday convenient? Then he went on to suggest they make an evening of it, because he felt like cooking. He would bring the groceries, and would one of them call him back to arrange a pickup? Good, Frederick thought, a visit from Jim was something they all looked forward to. He looked up at the kitchen clock. Olympia should be getting home any minute.

Sometimes she was ravenous when she got back from church. Other times she ate so much at the coffee hour, all she could do was pass through the kitchen on her way to a horizontal rendezvous with her latest book and a big soft pillow. He decided to wait and see rather than start something she might not finish. Usually he could tell by the way she entered the house. Marriage does that for you, he thought with a contented smile. You began to know your partner almost as well as you know yourself. Well, maybe not in Olympia's case. While not a woman of total mystery, she certainly was full of surprises. He rinsed out the electric tea kettle, which had been a wedding gift, and set it to boil. Whatever her state of mind, hot tea would be welcome on this bright, cold day.

Frederick didn't have long to wait. The water had just begun to boil when his lady love sailed in through the kitchen door. He held up the kettle and waved it in her direction.

"Love some herb, please, but first I have to make a phone call."

Olympia tossed her coat and hat in the general direction of the nearest kitchen chair and went straight through to her desk. There she pulled a church directory from under the nearest pile of papers, opened it to the A's and picked up her phone.

"Hi, Catherine, this is Olympia Brown calling. Have you got a minute?"

"I do indeed. In fact, I was just about to call you. It seems we have a little problem, and I'm not at all sure what to do about it."

"What kind of problem?"

"Well, it involves Emily Goodale. It's not the first time she's stirred things up around here, so I'm not inclined to take her assumptions and accusations to heart, but on the other hand, this one could have some serious implications."

Olympia could feel her stomach knotting. This was not what she wanted to hear. "What are you talking about, Catherine?"

"When I got home from church today, I had an e-mail from Emily. She is accusing you of making unwanted sexual advances toward her last night after the kids left and you both were alone."

"What!" shrieked Olympia.

"Not only did she send it to me, she sent copies to every member of the board."

"Oh, Jesus."

"You say something, my love?"

Olympia turned to see Frederick standing outside the bedroom door, holding up a cup of tea and pointing to it. Olympia shook her head, waved him off while mouthing the word "later" and pointed to the phone.

"Needless to say, I don't believe a word of it," Catherine continued, "and given her history with us, neither does anyone else, but she's never gone this far before. Usually she has a tiff with one person or another, and then she'll stalk around not speaking to them for a while, and that's about it. What in the world happened last night?"

Olympia blew out a long sigh. "Catherine, I'd like to talk to you in person. Something did happen last night, and I've already written it up and reported it to my District Supervisor. I was trying to catch you at church today to tell you, but you got away before I could. Do you have any time today? Can I meet you somewhere around the Bridge for an hour or so? There's an ice cream and coffee shop on the Cape side right after the exit. That would only be about a twenty-minute drive for each of us. Meeting at the church is out of the question."

Catherine was no fool and could tell by the sound of Olympia's voice that this situation needed their combined immediate attention.

"I can do that. Meet you in an hour? And if you don't mind, can you tell me what did happen last night?"

"I'll give you the full story, and a copy of the report when I see you, but the short form is, it was Emily that came on to me, not the other way around."

"Oh, dear," said Catherine.

"I'll tell you what. It might be good if you can bring another board member with you. We should move quickly in case Emily decides to go even more public with it."

"Good God, what are you talking about? What on earth else could she possibly do that's worse than this?"

"Bring in the police."

Now it was Catherine's turn to say, "Jesus!"

When she returned to the kitchen, Olympia went straight for the hat and coat she'd just taken off and began pulling them back on.

Frederick was holding out the still-hot mug of tea. "That didn't sound very good, my love."

"Can I have it in a travel mug, love? And in answer to your spoken question, some highly felonious shit has just hit the Salt Rock fan, and I'm afraid it's going to splatter everyone and everything in sight. Remember my telling you that Emily Goodale came on to me last night?"

He nodded.

"Well, she's turned it totally around and written to every member of the board, accusing me of sexual misconduct. She said I approached her at the church last night after the kids left and we were alone in my office."

"Crikey," said Frederick.

"I'm going to meet with Catherine and hopefully another board member right now. She doesn't believe it for a minute, and she knows Emily has attachment issues, but this is a new one for her, too."

"Do you want me to come along? I had some experience with this when I worked at the college. That was before we met. Perhaps I never told you."

Olympia allowed herself a moment of respite and glimpse of hope. "I didn't know that, and I will call upon you, just not yet. These people don't know you. Let me start on my own, and then, if need be, I can call you in when the time is right. Thank you, my dear and wonderful soul mate, thank you."

With that, she was out the door and humming down the drive toward the Sagamore Bridge, sipping at a travel mug full of lemon and ginger tea.

Twenty-Two

After Olympia's agitated departure Frederick didn't quite know what do with himself. He was far too distracted by the recent turn of events to do anything that might require precision or sharp tools. This left him with two options: a book and/or a nap. If he timed it right, one would segue neatly into the other. He was heading for the sitting room when he was stopped in his tracks by a strangled squawking sound emanating from the antique clock on the mantel over the stove. This was not a good omen. The clock had been discovered right after Olympia moved into the house when she was cleaning out a secret wall cupboard next to the fireplace. It had never worked properly, as in telling time, but it worked very well as a communication device for Miss Leanna Faith Winslow, their resident house ghost. When it made dissonant and guttural noises, as it just had, it usually meant something was amiss, proceed with caution—or in some cases, do not proceed at all.

Frederick looked at the clock. "I hear you, Madame, but what can I do? She's driving like a bat out of hell to an undisclosed destination." Then he remembered that Olympia was planning to have a conversation with people who would be on her side. Surely that was a good move, was it not? Nonetheless, forewarned is forearmed, and he would make sure to tell her that Miss Winslow had expressed concern. With that sorted, now he could flatten out with a book. Some people curled up with a book, but that never made sense to Frederick. Lots of things the Americans did made no sense to

Frederick, and rugged individual that he was, he would not conform. Frederick was English, and he had his little ways.

As she drove toward the bridge, and despite the anxiety surrounding the upcoming meeting, Olympia found herself thinking about Eileen Sullivan and wondering how she was doing. It would not be right to call and ask how the father of the child had reacted to the news, but she couldn't help wondering. Maybe she'd send her a "thinking about you" card to let her know just that. She did think about her, often.

She reached the coffee shop ahead of Catherine and took a booth as far away from the rest of the customers as she could manage. Since it was the middle of the afternoon, business was light, and there was no problem finding a place where they would not be overheard. Minutes after the cup of coffee she ordered arrived, Catherine Allen and Thom Whitehead, another member of the board, came through the door and joined her. After the greetings were completed, Catherine wasted no time in getting to the point.

"I brought Thom along because he's a member of the board and a retired school psychologist. He knows Emily and knew her parents, so he's got some background information."

She held out a printed copy of Emily's e-mail. "Here, this is the e-mail she sent to the board."

To Catherine Allen, Board President, and members of the Salt Rock Fellowship Parish Board.

Last night (Saturday) after the youth group left the building and I was alone with Reverend Brown in her office, she came up to me and put her hand on my breast and made a disgusting suggestion.

I had my suspicions about her when she kept inviting me into her office for private conversations. At first I thought she was taking an interest in me because I told her I was having trouble making friends, but now I know it was more than that. MUCH MORE. UGH!

I didn't know what to do, so I just said no and got out of there as fast as I could, but when I got home I couldn't sleep and I knew I had to do something before she goes after someone else. If you think about it, she DID VOLUNTEER to do that bake sale, didn't she? NOW YOU KNOW WHY!

I know it's my word against hers, but with GOD AS MY JUDGE, she's a sick evil person and she needs to be STOPPED!

I don't know what you plan to do, but I for one will swear on a Bible that this happened.

What kind of a church would keep someone like that on the payroll anyway? You have to ask yourselves that question.

I'm not coming back until that woman is gone...and another thing, if she goes after anyone else, like a defenseless child, you bear the blame as much as her.

Emily Goodale.

Olympia pushed away the cup of coffee and handed the sheet of paper back to Catherine. She sat for a moment and looked across the table at the two of them. Would they be advocates or accusers, she wondered? Their solemn faces gave no indication.

Catherine was the first to speak. "The woman has been difficult ever since she started coming to Salt Rock. She gets all cozy with someone, and then one day it's a total about-face and she's badmouthing them. It's no wonder people stay away from her." Catherine held up the e-mail. "I don't believe it for a minute, not one word."

"We all know she's difficult, but what would make her do something as vicious as this?" asked Thom.

"Reverend Phil had problems with her, too, I knew that," said Catherine.

"May I speak?" said Olympia.

"Of course," said Catherine.

"Actually, before I say anything, I would like one of you to take notes on this conversation. The first thing I did was to call Phil Rutledge. I told him everything and asked if he wanted to be involved personally. He said not yet, that I was doing all the right things, and I should contact you, Catherine, and keep him informed. After speaking with him I reported the incident to my District Supervisor and then wrote a detailed description of exactly what happened. I intended to bring it with me, but I left the house in such a rush I forgot. I will get you a copy tomorrow."

"You could e-mail it," said Thom.

"If it's all the same, I'd rather not. E-mails can get derailed. I'll give you a hard copy."

He shrugged. "Suit yourself."

"I'll take notes," said Catherine, pulling a pencil and a note pad out of her purse. "Now, in your own words tell us what happened,"

Before she could begin, a waitress came up to the table and took their orders; a regular decaf coffee and a large hot chocolate. After she left Olympia carefully and explicitly described the events leading up to Saturday night. She started with Emily's phone call to her at home in late December, right after she signed the contract with the church. She went on to describe the succession of gifts, starting with the flower left on her desk on her first Sunday in the pulpit. Then she ticked off on her fingers the lavender, the chocolate, the smelly candle and the constant offers of coffee and personal assistance whenever the opportunity presented itself.

Whitehead cleared his throat. "I must say that none of those gestures seem particularly troubling, Reverend. They're little more than thoughtful tokens of appreciation from a member of the congregation. Lots of people do that. Frankly, I don't see a problem so far."

Olympia willed herself not to fidget or wiggle her foot, something she did when she was agitated or irritated, and she was beginning to be a little of both. She hadn't thought she'd be speaking in her own defense, but it was beginning to feel that way. Then there was the confidentiality issue. How much would she say? How much *could* she say? The gifts were public knowledge. Charlotte had witnessed them all. She took a deep breath and began again.

"In and of themselves, Thom, the gifts really are insignificant. Ordinarily I'd just smile and say thank you, but this is different. She actually called me at home before I started work here. From that first conversation it has been clear to me that she was one of those people who would need care and attention. I'm afraid the gifts were her way of trying to win my approval. It happens. I tried repeatedly to make her understand that I liked her for who she was, and she didn't need to bring me things to thank me for simply doing my job. We do our best, but that may have been the wrong thing to say to her. If you don't mind, I want to get back to what happened Saturday night."

"Of course," said Thom.

"I asked Emily to help out with the kids on Saturday as a way to help her find a healthy place in the congregation, not in a one-on-one with me, but in a noisy and natural group setting where she'd be a real help."

"And was she?" asked Catherine.

"She was indeed. Other than sticking pretty close to me, which I attributed to nervousness around all those teenagers, she did a great job. She's a natural in the kitchen. I really thought I'd made some progress helping her fit in."

"Then what?" said Thom.

"When everyone had left, and we were alone in the kitchen, she came up behind me and kissed me on the back of the neck. I must have jumped three feet in the air. I was totally shocked."

"What did you do then?" Now he was taking notes.

"I told her to come into my office with the intention of setting her straight right then and there, but once we were inside the office, her advances became more direct. When I tried to pull away, she held on to my hand, saying what did I expect, that I was the one who'd encouraged her. When I denied that and said we needed to have another conversation, she grabbed her things and took off. I have to tell you, I didn't sleep very well last night."

"I don't blame you," said Catherine.

"And now what?" said Thom.

Olympia shook her head. "I'm not exactly sure, but whatever it is, we need to be in complete agreement before I set foot back in the church."

Whitehead leaned back in his chair and looked at Olympia over his glasses. "On the other hand, maybe you'd best not set foot back in the church."

Olympia could keep her foot from wiggling, but she could not control the rush of blood to her cheeks. "What are you talking about? Surely you don't believe what's in that e-mail?"

He began tapping the table with his fingertips. "Right now, without material evidence or a witness, it's her word against yours. Believe me, I've had experience with this sort of thing. What we sometimes would do is put the accused person on administrative leave with pay until it can be sorted out."

Olympia was wide eyed and open mouthed. "Accused? What are you talking about? I'm the victim! That woman came on to me. Are you telling me I can't go to work?"

"Yes and no. In this day and age it's possible to work from home. I'm suggesting that henceforth you never be in the church alone, only when the administrator is there, or there's a meeting going on, or you are there for the Sunday service. This is for your protection, not Emily's."

Olympia relaxed. "Okay, I think I see where you're going with this."

He smiled. "Good. I don't believe it for a minute either, but people like that can be very dangerous, and I'm not talking about the cohesion of the congregation here. I'm talking about you, Olympia. You see, I've known her family for years. Like I said, I knew her parents. Emily has been in and out of psychiatric hospitals for as long as I can remember. She's delusional, poor thing, but she has long periods of reasonably normal behavior, so it's easy to forget she's ill. Then all of a sudden, something sets her off, and she falls apart. I think she stops taking her meds. People do that, you know. People who need medication to function normally will, for no apparent reason, suddenly stop taking them, and then all hell breaks loose."

"Would there be any benefit to getting in touch with her parents?" asked Olympia.

"Not possible. It was one of the bigger news items around here a couple of years ago. They're both dead. According to the published report it was a murder-suicide. There were questions, of course, but no one actually pressed charges. It's not all that uncommon. One elderly spouse is terminally ill, and the other is overwhelmed with the care-giving. It's terribly sad. She may be in her forties, but Emily is an orphan, and I think that's a contributing factor."

Olympia nodded. "So what exactly are you suggesting?"

"Be available but cautiously present. When you need to connect with people, do it by phone and e-mail, and don't ever be alone in the church until we decide on the best course of action for all concerned."

"Are you telling me she might try and hurt me?"

"I don't think so. She's delusional, not homicidal. Mostly she's sad and frightened, thinks everyone dislikes her and is out to get her. I don't want you to be in any sort of position or situation where she might have the opportunity to make another accusation."

"It's that serious, then?" said Olympia.

"Let's just say forewarned is forearmed."

"My mother used to say that all the time."

"Its good advice," said Thomas Whitehead.

Twenty-Three

By the time she'd shucked her heavy winter clothing and accepted the cup of tea Frederick held out to her, Olympia was feeling considerably better than she had been earlier in the day. As they sat together at the kitchen table sipping their tea and working through a plate of ginger cookies, she related the latest developments in the Emily-saga. The good news was that she was beginning to see the situation in its larger perspective, a woman suffering with mental illness, instead of taking it as a personal attack.

Rather than having misread the signals and caused the problem herself, Olympia began to understand that she was simply the nearest moving target. If it hadn't been her, then it would have been someone else. More importantly, Frederick agreed with her and was actually pleased with Catherine and Thom's recommendation that she continue in place but take care never to be alone in the church until the matter was fully resolved.

"I suggest you call or e-mail your District Supervisor and let him know where things stand. The more people in the management loop that know about this, the better for you."

Olympia smiled. "It's next on my list. It sounds odd to hear you use the term management loop, Frederick, but I suppose when I think about it, that's exactly what it is."

"My dear," Frederick arched a superior eyebrow in her direction, "I haven't bothered to mention it to you before this, because I thought it to be self-evident, but like it or not, from what I have observed, churches are very similar to businesses.

Organizations are organizations, no matter which way you slice them. Of course, we could quarrel about who or what might be the CEO, but for the most part, churches are largely governed by money and power. A skillful minister knows that and knows how to negotiate the rapids without making too many waves."

"I have the feeling I'm running ahead of a tsunami with this one, my love, but after this afternoon, I feel these people believe me and support me. I suppose the next step is to try and get someone to help poor Emily. By the sound of it, she's way out of control."

Frederick held up his hand. "Hold it right there, sunshine. Your job is to protect yourself first, and then, with the help of the board and your supervisor, deal with Emily. You said her parents are both dead, so that complicates things a bit. That could be part of the problem."

"How so?"

"We don't know if there are any siblings or other relatives who might be able to step in and help or at least offer advice. Without that, she's just out there doing heaven only knows what. Do you see what I mean? There's no support system."

Olympia nodded thoughtfully as Thunderfoot pawed his way onto her lap. She considered telling Frederick about the death of Emily's parents. The disturbing story of a murder-suicide and the questions surrounding it might all be part of the larger picture, but they were not particularly relevant in this conversation, so she left it unsaid. But relevant or not, the whole thing was pretty damned unsettling, and Olympia Brown didn't like being unsettled. It was not good for her appetite. Respond to the question, Olympia!

"Mmm, good point, and I will duly consider all of it, but as of this moment, there's not a thing I can do about *any* of it. Therefore, I suggest we raid the fridge for a quick grab and growl supper, then go into the next room and work our way to the bottom of that sea chest."

"Grab and growl supper?" asked Frederick.

"That's when all you have is leftovers, and you put them all out on the table, and may the best and fastest man, or woman, in this case, win. The freshest and tastiest ones always go first. Hence, grab and growl."

"Check," said Frederick.

Outside in the dark, Emily Goodale was watching the two of them through a set of high-powered binoculars. She'd parked her car in such a way that she could see straight down the driveway and in through the kitchen window. She wished she could read their lips and know what they were talking about, but that would be asking too much. Right now it was enough just to know where Olympia was and what she was doing.

Frederick and Olympia were putting away the supper dishes when the phone rang and startled both of them. In unspoken agreement they waited until they heard Jim's voice before Olympia picked up.

"Hi, Jim, did I hear you were coming down this week to borrow back your car?"

"You did indeed. I want to get it back into a covered garage in Boston before we get that snowstorm on Wednesday."

"If we get it, Jim. This far out, they really can't be all that precise, you know."

"Better safe than sorry, Olympia, and either way, I need the car for a couple of days."

"Why don't you come down on Tuesday and spend the night? That way we can relax, have a good meal and catch up."

"That works. I need to check my hospital schedule first. That one is more flexible than the teaching schedule. I can put in my hours in the morning, and that way I'll miss the traffic."

Olympia smiled into the phone. Jim was her dearest friend and just hearing his voice lifted her weary spirit. When he was there, she would take the opportunity to ask his advice on the Emily saga. She wondered whether he'd ever had this kind of thing happen to him, and if so, what he'd done about it.

"Frederick will be home all day on Tuesday, so call and let us know when you need to be picked up."

Olympia replaced the receiver and joined Frederick and the cats in the sitting room.

"I checked the weather report while you were on the phone. If we do get that storm, it's going to be pretty bad. I'll go out tomorrow and get the necessaries while you're at the church. I'll also lay in a good supply of wood both inside and outside right next to the kitchen door. That way we'll be prepared for any eventuality."

"Pure genius, Frederick. What would I do without you?"

"Well, if memory serves, I seem to recall your taking care of yourself pretty well in a massive storm some years back. We were telephone-courting at the time, and I was frightfully concerned for your welfare."

She nodded. "It was an incredible storm, all right, scary as hell. We had high wind and snow and no power for almost a week, and my first-born got himself stranded with a bunch of religious loonies on the other side of Boston. That was some storm in more ways than one."

Frederick sat back on his heels, held up an expository index finger and began to speak.

*When icicles hang by the wall, and Dick the shepherd
blows his nail,
  And Tom bears logs into the hall, and milk comes
frozen home in pail;
When blood be nipt and ways be foul,
Then nightly sings the staring owl,
Tu-whoo!
Tu-whit! To-whoo! A merry note
While greasy Joan doth keel the pot.*

"William Shakespeare, *Love's Labour's Lost*."

"Shakespeare may be timeless, my love, but when all is said and done, 'When blood be nipt and ways be foul,'" Olympia flicked a lascivious wink in his direction, "I'd rather be stoking the midnight fire with a sexy, balding Englishman."

Frederick's answering leer spoke volumes. "Maybe later, dearie. Right now, you and I have a date with a sea chest. I've waited long enough."

With Frederick and Olympia no longer in view, Emily considered getting out of the car and walking closer to the house, but the bitter cold was getting to her, and she was starting to shiver. After putting the binoculars back into the glove compartment, she cupped her hands and blew on them to get some blood and warmth back into her fingers before driving off into the night. On the passenger seat beside her lay her "Reverend Olympia" notebook. She took it everywhere with her now.

Two hours later Olympia lifted the last of the long-hidden treasures into the light and breathed a dusty, sneezy sigh of relief. The trunk was empty. Mostly they'd found packets of papers which at first glance looked like more household records. There were a few items of men's and women's clothing, in too much disrepair to be of any value other than historic curiosity, and much to Olympia's delight, another sepia toned photograph, crumbling at the corners. She took it out and held it under the light. The face was that of the woman in the locket, older now but comfortingly familiar. How I wish you could speak, Olympia thought, but I suppose, in your own way, you do.

"What cheek. Would you look at those two," said Frederick, pointing in the direction of the empty trunk where two cat faces could be seen peering over the edge.

"If I weren't so tired I'd be charmed, but the truth is I'm, dead on my feet, or in this case, on my butt. I'm going to bed, darling, if I can walk that far."

"I'll join you shortly, I just want to sift through a bit more of this clutter before I turn in. In some ways it's like a book I can't put down. I know there's more in here and just a little bit more."

"And a little bit more after that. Don't be too late, darling. You'll pay for it in the morning."

March 22, 1863
It has been some weeks since I have taken pen in hand, and now I write, for there is so much to say. This winter's deadly hold on us has finally broken. My garden crocuses braved the chilly winds of March and blessed us with abundant color and the certainty of coming spring. On the day of that first real warmth we opened the doors and the windows to enjoy the fragrant air, and my blessed Aunt Louisa breathed her last with a smile on her face. Jonathan still runs into her bedroom and then turns back and asks

"Whereweeza?" I tell him she was very old and tired, so she decided to die. It is a truth he will one day understand.

The day after we laid her to rest, a letter arrived with the news that my novel is to be published. Joy overrides my sadness for a time, but then I remember that I cannot run and tell her my good news. Perhaps she knows. I try to comfort myself with such thoughts. More anon, LFW

Twenty-Four

As tempted as she was to stay home and pick through the disparate contents of the sea chest still scattered around the sitting room, Olympia's sense of duty prevailed. She bundled herself up, got into Jim's car and headed south to the church. If they did find themselves snowbound later in the week, it would be a perfect way to spend a winter afternoon, sitting by the fire and learning more firsthand about the history of the house.

On a Monday morning in February on the Upper Cape, there is little to no traffic to contend with, and Olympia had a clear shot. Jim's car might have a few years on it, but the luxury of warmth at the touch of a button, and a good radio blasting Mozart out of both speakers, gave her no reason to hurry. She decided to turn off at the first exit and take Route 6A, the more picturesque road that ran almost parallel to the main highway. To complete this self-indulgent meander, she turned into the parking lot of Titcomb's Bookshop for a browse and maybe a little retail therapy. She loved the friendly people, the interesting selection and even the quirky building. It was the kind of temptation that she, a proper minister, never considered resisting. After that she stopped at a drive-through coffee shop for a cappuccino, cranked the Mozart up a little further and slipped into her day. She had no idea what or who might be waiting for her when she reached her destination, but come what may, the Reverend Doctor Olympia Brown was off to a good start.

Back in Brookfield, Frederick was getting ready to go to the bookstore. After his second cup of tea he did a quick tour around the house, making sure the cats had food and water, the lights were turned off and the heat turned down. He looked forward to going to work. He loved books, he adored Betsey D., the owner, and he enjoyed helping the succession of parents and children who came in during the day. Some of them came to select a special treasure, and others came just to sit on one of the big comfy chairs and share a book together.

He looked around at the big, inconvenient, outdated kitchen, the uneven walls and the multi-paned windows. Every time he had to leave this rambling piece of New England history that had become his home, he felt a twinge of longing to stay. The house had a soul and a personality, and he, Frederick Watkins, had appointed himself its protector and caretaker. Side by side, he and Olympia were literally sifting through its history, one box and one splintery board and one rusted hinge at a time.

He stepped outside into the bright, biting cold and looked up at the sky. No snow clouds or high, thin overcast as of yet, just another brilliant winter's day in his new land. I could get used to this, he thought, and then he corrected himself. I am used to this, and I bloody well love it, he thought.

Despite the drama of the last two days, Olympia was feeling cheerful and looking forward to a quiet morning. She had some pastoral calls to make in the afternoon, and there were a few things to take care of in the office before she set off. Her meeting with Catherine Allen and Thom Whitehead had assured her they were on her side and that Emily had a difficult history, which they knew about and understood. While not exactly comforting, Olympia did not feel as if she were trying to deal with this situation all on her own. What she didn't know was how much Charlotte knew or how much she should tell her.

What am I thinking? she asked herself. Charlotte knows everything around here, doesn't she? In fact, wasn't it she who told me that Emily had issues in the first place? The more she thought about it, the more it made sense to tell her everything. Charlotte was often the interface between her and the parishioners, and if Emily came in and started acting out, it would definitely help if she knew what was going on. With that settled, she was ready to begin her day. A good thing it was, too, because she was already at the church with little recollection of having driven there. Gotta watch that stuff, she told herself.

Once she was in and settled, she was pleased to learn there was nothing needing her immediate attention. Also, there were a few little goodies left over from Sunday morning. After all, the remains of the double cappuccino needed something to keep it company. Just as she was about to go and tell Charlotte about the events of Saturday and Sunday, the phone rang. It was Eileen Sullivan. Olympia got up from her desk and quietly closed the door to her office.

"Hi, Eileen. I've been thinking about you. How are you feeling?"

"Pretty good. Still kind of nauseated, but not as bad as it was." She paused. "I told Jimmy about the baby."

"What was his response?" Olympia could feel her neck and shoulder muscles tensing.

"First off, he didn't say anything, just sat and stared at the floor."

"Then what happened?"

"He asked if I wanted to get married; I told you he was a nice guy. But I told him no. I said getting married just to give the baby a name was not, in my mind, a good reason."

"How did he respond to that?"

"At first he didn't say anything. He was almost crying. Then he said he'd do anything I needed him to do, and he hoped we could go on seeing each other, because he really cared about me. I told him I was okay with that, but since I was still getting used to the idea of having a baby at all, I didn't know what I might need."

"What do your parents think about the arrangement?"

Eileen groaned. "They're all over the place. They tell me they'll support me whatever I do, but I think they would really like it if I married Jimmy. But I don't want to, at least not now."

"It's a lot to think about, Eileen. I think you are handling it very well."

"Thanks to you, Reverend."

Olympia smiled into the phone. "I'm here if you need me any time. Remember that."

"I will, Reverend, thank you."

"When you think about it, give me a call or shoot me an e-mail once in a while and let me know how you are doing."

"I don't want to make a pest of myself."

"Not possible, Eileen. We've got some history now, so keep me in the loop. You'll never be a pest."

When she finished with the call, she got up, stretched and walked out into Charlotte's office only to be greeted by Forrest Marsh.

"Good morning, Forrest!" she yelled.

He had already taken off his coat and was making himself comfortable in the visitor's chair. "I was driving by, and I thought I'd come in to make sure you girls are all set for the storm on Wednesday."

Charlotte and Olympia exchanged glances, but it was Olympia who responded.

"We are going to leave before it starts, and my husband is out right now getting supplies!"

"What?"

"We'll be okay!" screamed Charlotte.

He reached into his pocket and pulled out a plastic grocery sack. "I brought you these just in case. Plumber candles, they burn forever. Three each and matches, too. Nobody smokes these days, so matches are hard to find."

Olympia blinked back the tears and reached for the candles. "Thank you so much, Forrest!" she hollered. Then she carefully counted out three for herself and three for Charlotte.

"I may be a living relic, but I do know how to get by in a storm. You girls be careful now. I need to get gas before I go home."

Olympia winced at the thought of him driving but tactfully kept it to herself.

After he left, the two women had a companionable giggle, and then Olympia got serious. She filled Charlotte in on the Emily saga, as she thought of it, and the need for her never to be alone in the church until the matter was resolved.

Charlotte shook her head. "I knew she had problems, but I had no idea it was this bad. On the other hand, maybe it's just getting worse as she gets older. Did you tell Reverend Phil?"

"Oh, yes. That was the first call I made after telling my District Supervisor. Keeping silent is the worst thing you can do in a situation like this, but you can't exactly broadcast if from the bell tower either. It's enough that you and I and the board know. She may start talking to other people, but we don't have any control over that."

"Poor thing," said Charlotte. She was biting her lip and shaking her head.

Poor dangerous thing, thought Olympia, and then she heard it again, shadowy organ music coming from the sanctuary.

"Did you hear that?"

Charlotte grinned and nodded. "Yup, that's old Jeremy. He's been a bit noisy of late. I wonder what's got his attention. Must be you. Seems like Forrest isn't the only old guy in this place with an eye for the ladies."

Olympia rolled her eyes. "You know, if we put this stuff in a book, no one would believe us."

"But it is in a book—a couple, in fact. Every so often somebody decides to write another book on Cape Cod ghosts and haunted houses. Salt Rock and our Jeremy always make the final cut. Living here as long as I have, you get used to it, I suppose. It comes with the territory. Old buildings lead a double life. At least, they do around here."

"You're preaching to the choir, Charlotte. My recently acquired old house came with a ghost. I even know her name. It's Miss Leanna Faith Winslow."

"Maybe you should introduce her to Jeremy."

Olympia giggled. "I'll try not to think of the possibilities—but right now, duty calls. I want to make my pastoral visits before Wednesday, especially with the elderly. While I'm visiting I can check to make sure they have emergency plans and provisions in place. If the storm is as bad as some are predicting, I want to know who and where they are if they need help."

"Good woman," said Charlotte.

"I try," said Olympia.

Outside the church, Emily did a turn through the parking lot and made note of the fact that Olympia was driving that other car, the Toyota. For some reason seeing this made her uncomfortable, even irritable. It wasn't predictable.

That evening, while Frederick was nodding over a crossword, and Olympia was about to tackle another box of papers that had come out of the sea chest, the phone rang. It was Laura.

"Hi, Mom. I'm calling to wish you a happy Valentine's Day."

"Well, thank you, dear, and the same to you. I'm afraid I haven't sent any cards or anything. You kind of get out of that after a while. Besides, it's not until Wednesday. I suppose a good grandmother would at least send one to her granddaughter, but I failed that test, too. You and Gerry doing anything special to celebrate it?"

"Funny you should ask. I guess maybe that's really why I called."

"Okay, honey, I'm asking. How are you and Gerry going to celebrate?"

"By getting engaged. We're going to give each other rings that we'll use as our wedding rings when we get married."

Olympia caught her breath and squealed softly so as not to wake Frederick, who was now purring quietly into his chest. "Oh, honey, that's wonderful. Have you told your other mother?"

"I called her this morning. She's happy, too."

"As I remember, same sex marriage isn't legal in California yet, so I guess you'll just have to come east so I can perform the ceremony—that is, if you'd like me to."

"First things first, Mother, but yes, that is the plan. We thought sometime this summer. I get three weeks' vacation. I thought we could spend a week with my adoptive parents in Winchester and a week with you and Frederick. Then maybe we could leave Erica with one set of grandparents while Gerry and I go off by ourselves for a couple of days."

Olympia was finding it difficult to talk around her face-splitting grin and the lump in her throat. "Oh, honey, that is the best. Pick a day, any day, and we'll be here. It will be fun planning a wedding with your other mother. Does poor Gerry know she's getting not one but two mothers-in-law on your side of the family?"

"And both mothers-in-law are getting a second daughter. It works both ways, Mother dear."

When Frederick came to, his pencil still in his hand and his cup of tea ice cold on the coffee table in front of him, Olympia told him the good news and asked if he was ready for another wedding in the family.

"To be honest, my love, the way I see it, weddings are girl things. What I'm looking forward to is being a grandpa for a few weeks. You ladies can deal with the tea and the cakes and the assorted festivities, and leave the little one to me."

Twenty-Five

By Tuesday all predictions were for a major snowstorm on Wednesday, possibly one of historic proportions. The only variations were how major and how historic, but all were agreed that it would be nothing to take lightly. Olympia and Frederick, along with everyone else on the southeast coast of New England, were in storm prep mode. They were gathering and stacking wood and laying in an ample supply of people food and cat food, bottled water and decent wine. They were joined by literally hundreds of their friends and neighbors, chasing around to stores with rapidly emptying shelves, looking for batteries, more candles, matches and lamp oil.

Tuesday was not ordinarily a day when Charlotte was in the office at church, but because of the forecast, she and Olympia decided to work Tuesday, and even Wednesday morning, if need be, so they could have everything taken care of on the church front. Then they would do as advised: go home, stay off the roads and maybe even have a chance to use the plumber's candles.

Meanwhile, it was a regular morning of phone calls, some fact-checking for her upcoming sermon and then a local clergy meeting. A day like every day in the life of me, she thought, and it was beginning to feel almost normal.

In her own modest home, a drafty winter rental about ten minutes from the church, Emily Goodale was making her own preparations. In terms of her larger objective, the one concerning Reverend Olympia Brown, the impending storm was going to be a major interruption. It would no doubt delay what she had so carefully constructed. Delay, but not destroy, since Emily always had a Plan B. "To everything there is a season, and a time to every purpose under heaven," she reminded herself. Emily knew how to bide her time. She'd done it once before, and everything had worked out just the way it was supposed to. Meanwhile, she needed to get herself to work. She'd traded days with one of the other girls so she could have Wednesday off, and to keep up her end of the deal it was important to show up on time. Order and dependability counted for a lot as far as she was concerned.

By the time Olympia was driving home on Tuesday afternoon, even though nothing was supposed to happen until the following afternoon, the first wispy clouds heralding the coming storm began to slide in from the northeast. As she drove along the back roads she kept replaying in her head the conversation with her daughter of the night before, the engagement, a wedding, seeing her daughter and her granddaughter again, meeting Gerry. It was the stuff of more happiness than she had ever envisioned for herself as far as her daughter was concerned.

"I don't know who or what you are or where you might be, but thank you, God," she whispered. Before she knew it, she was home and crunching up the driveway. She pulled in close beside Frederick's truck and hopped out of the car. Jim would be there, and she was anxious to see him. She expected him to stay the night. He often did when the wine flowed freely, and he didn't have to be at work too early, but there was the storm to consider. If he didn't have to be out at the crack of dawn, he might stay on for that, as well. What fun, she thought, snowbound with my cats, my two favorite men, a roaring fire and a good bottle of wine, or two, or three. How good is that? It was a rhetorical question.

Jim was already standing at the kitchen stove when Olympia arrived. The smells of butter, garlic and wine could not be contained by a mere storm door. Olympia followed her nose to the source and gave her best friend a big, cold-faced kiss.

"Mmm, what is it?" she said, peering into the sizzling skillet.

"Shrimp scampi for the Englishman and myself and mushroom scampi with capers for the lady."

"Is that all?" Olympia was unwinding herself from her multiple winter layers.

"Aren't we the greedy little minister?" laughed Jim. "To which I will add a mélange of spring greens tossed with a reduced balsamic vinaigrette, hot crusty bread and something to surprise you for dessert, or pudding, as that man over there has taught me to say."

"Glass of wine, my love?" asked Frederick.

She held out her hand. "Yes, please. You going to stay on for the storm, Jim?"

"If it's not too much trouble. Beacon Hill is impossible to negotiate on the best of days. Add a foot or two of snow to that, and the place goes into total lockdown. If I'm going to be stranded, which by all reports, I'm likely to be, I might as well be stranded with friends, *n'est-ce pas?*"

"Oooooh, I do love it when you talk dirty, Jim." Olympia was delighted. It was all working out the way she'd hoped.

After dinner Olympia volunteered for clean-up while the two men restocked the wood and kindling supply. Speaking of storm prep, even Frederick, while not a whiz in the kitchen, did have a few standbys. Earlier in the day he'd made a giant vegetable curry, which he'd left to rest in the unheated back entry for twenty-four hours to let the flavors mature.

Later, when they'd decided they were as prepared as they cared to be, Olympia filled them both in on the Emily saga. In so doing she earned both their concern and their sympathy for the difficulty of the situation and the delicacy needed to handle it.

"I've had both men and women come on to me," said Jim, "but I never felt threatened. Usually a clarifying conversation was enough to take care of it. I can't imagine what I'd do if this happened to me."

"I'll tell you, Jim, it ain't lovely, but I do have the support of everyone I've told, so that's something. I just feel sorry for Emily."

"Don't feel that sorry, Olympia. This Emily person may be unhinged, but you're still in the crosshairs."

"I hear you, my love, and I am being really careful, but it's still sad. Poor thing."

"And now for something completely different," said Jim. He'd gone out into the kitchen and was now standing in the doorway, holding a totally decadent, pink and white frosted, double chocolate Valentine's Day cake "to celebrate tomorrow."

"Ohhh, yeah," said Olympia.

By Wednesday morning, Valentine's Day, things felt almost normal. With the ordinariness of routine tasks filling her time, Olympia didn't jump when the phone rang or she heard a knock at the door. She no longer felt anxious if she heard an unfamiliar sound, and she wasn't checking the rear view mirror at every bend in the road.

Earlier in the week, the Parish Board met without Olympia in attendance. Together they worked out a plan to invite Emily in to discuss the contents of the e-mail with two or three members of the board, her choice, and if she wished, Zak Bilecki, the District Supervisor. They hoped this could take place before the end of the week, but at this point everything on anyone's calendar in New England was followed by the words, "weather permitting."

Cape Codders knew all about coastal storms, and they knew how to deal with them. After all, they'd been doing it for generations. The one thing they all agreed on was that Mother Nature holds all the cards, and you don't take chances. Be prepared, stay off the roads, and if possible, make hot soup.

Forecasters were cautiously pessimistic about the duration and intensity of the storm. Some were predicting gale force winds and twelve to eighteen inches of heavy, wet snow along the coast. Others were hinting that fifty miles one way or the other in the storm track could make a difference in an accumulation of feet, rather than inches, of snow. Either way, this would be a storm to be reckoned with. It was to begin, they said, in the early afternoon, starting with freezing rain and then ice turning to snow as the temperature dropped and the winds increased.

Olympia learned a new word that week: bombogenesis, which is what happens when a developing storm literally explodes within itself and grows into a monster. She remembered her mother telling her as a child about a deadly Valentine's Day blizzard from her own childhood and how terrifying it had been to be in a dark house with no heat. Also, the metaphoric parallel between the Emily saga and the approach of a menacing storm was not lost on Olympia.

But Olympia wasn't really worried about the coming blizzard. This was, after all, the twenty-first century, and she had a big old house that would keep her safe and warm. The truth was, she loved big, fat, hairy snowstorms; and with all her preparations and provisions firmly in place, she planned to hunker down and settle in for the duration.

Before that could happen, she had to go over the bridge and down to the church one more time so she could cross the t's and dot the i's for the coming Sunday. Once that was done, she could stay home for the rest of the week. This would also create a flexible timeframe for the board to meet with Emily later in the week with no possibility of Olympia or anyone else interrupting them.

Charlotte was already at her desk when a bright-eyed Olympia breezed into the office and stood stamping her feet and rubbing her hands. "Man, it's raw out there. I suppose it's worse down here, surrounded by water and everything. There's a definite snow feel to the air. It's unmistakable."

"We need to be out of here by noon or at the sight of the first flake, whichever comes first," said Charlotte.

"I thought it was supposed to start as rain."

"Okay, the first drop, then. First rain, then freezing rain, then ice, and then all hell breaks loose. I'm not waiting around."

"Nor am I," said Olympia. "This is really just to cover our bases so we don't have to come in for the rest of the week. Anything else I can do from home."

With that brief exchange, the two women sat down at their respective desks and set about clearing off and going through those things that needed attending to. It was only when she looked up that Olympia saw the tissue paper-stuffed gift bag hanging on the back of her door.

"Damn!" she spat and threw the pencil she was holding down onto the desk.

"Something I said?" called Charlotte.

"I only wish it was. I'll be out in a minute. I need to check something."

Olympia retrieved the gift with no doubt whatsoever in her mind as to who had left it. The question was when and how?

She lifted the thing off the doorknob with her thumb and forefinger and marched back to her desk. There she yanked out the pink and red tissue paper and shook out the contents. The latest gift was an unsigned children's penny valentine with the message "Forever Mine" and a dead white rose with its stem broken in half.

"Damn-damn-damn-damn-damn!" Olympia ranted as she stormed out into Charlotte's office.

"Excuse me, Reverend, but what the hell is going on?"

"By any chance, did Emily Goodale come in here before I arrived?"

"Not since I've been here. Why, what did you find in there?"

"She left me a valentine and a dead rose. Of course, she was too smart to sign the card, but there's no question who it's from. How in God's name did she get in here? That's what I'd like to know."

"That's creepy, and I'm afraid God had nothing to do with it. More than likely, she has a key. An awful lot of people have them, you know. I suppose we should keep a list."

"Meanwhile, what do I do?"

"Nothing. I'm here with you, and we're going home in less than an hour. I suggest you wrap it up and save it for the board as further evidence of what's she's doing. The poor thing is, well, you know, she's just not right."

"And getting worse," added Olympia. "Calling her and screaming at her would do no good at all, but that's exactly what I feel like doing."

"Well, don't. Go make a cup of coffee or something, and let's do those things which ought to be done, then get our behinds out of here before the fury begins."

"Preach on, sister," said Olympia.

Twenty-Six

Distracting herself by making the coffee turned out to be a good idea, and even better was finding the leftover coffee cake. She dutifully carried all of this back to the office and shared it with Charlotte. Now she was ready to finish up and call it a day.

Moments later Charlotte stuck her head in the door and waved at her. She was dressed for the oncoming weather.

"I'm done, and it's starting to sprinkle out there. I'm leaving, and I suggest you do the same."

Olympia waved back. "I'm almost done. I have to make one more phone call, but that will be no more than five minutes, I promise."

"Okay, then, but I'm going to lock the door behind me. We agreed that you wouldn't be alone here. If you want to, you can throw the deadbolt, and then God himself couldn't get in here."

"Herself!"

"You're sure of that, are you?"

"Consider it another holy mystery. Now get going. I'll be right behind you."

Olympia got up and followed Charlotte to the front door, and when it clicked shut, she slid the deadbolt into place. As she walked back to her office, the echo of her footsteps in the empty building made it sound as if someone was following her. She shivered. The temperature in the creaky old place was already dropping, and outside, the wind was picking up. Maybe she wouldn't make that phone call. Pellets of freezing rain were sliding down the windows. It was time to go home. She turned to go back to her desk and froze. Emily Goodale was standing in the doorway, smiling at her. Olympia froze. Keep calm, she told herself. The woman needs help, not anger.

"Emily, how did you get into my office without my knowing it?"

Emily pointed to the door behind her. "I have a key to the outside door in your office. It's really been quite useful."

Act normal, Olympia.

"I thought I was the only one to have that key. Seems I was wrong. Well, now that you're here, come in and tell me what's on your mind."

"You said you wanted to talk to me." Emily remained standing, her feet slightly apart and her hands crammed in her pockets. "Here I am."

"I told you I wanted to make a time for us to talk about what happened Saturday night, but instead, you sent an e-mail to the board with an entirely different version of what took place."

Olympia could hear the ice crystals coming faster now. They made a silvery patter against the windows and on the roof overhead.

"I had to. No one would believe me if I didn't."

"Emily, what you wrote about me is simply untrue, and you know it. We need to have an honest and caring conversation with each other, but it can't be just the two of us."

"Why is that, may I ask? Are you afraid of me, Reverend? Afraid to be alone with me? Afraid you might lose control?"

Olympia took in a long, slow, calming breath. "Emily, I want the best for you—for both of us really, but it can't happen in a one-on-one meeting without someone to help us communicate and understand each other. There's a killer snowstorm bearing down on both of us, and neither of us should be out in it."

"Fine!" Emily spat. "Have it your way, Reverend, but I'm coming back." With that, she whirled around, ran out the office door and slammed it viciously behind her.

Badly shaken, Olympia dropped into the nearest chair and took a few deep breaths as the storm outside intensified by the second. In what seemed no time at all, the ice and sleet had turned to snow and was starting to collect along the edges of the grass.

She wasted no time in gathering her things and piling on her winter clothing. Prudently, she'd brought along a pair of boots, which she pulled on and then declared herself ready to brave the elements. Futile though it might be, she locked the office door behind her and, head down against the wind, made her way across the empty parking lot to the van. The wind and snow were bad, but the walking was even worse. There was a layer of ice underneath the rapidly building snow, and she almost fell twice before she reached the safety of her van.

There was already an inch of snow on its windows and roof, and she would have to brush off before she could move. She pulled open the door and climbed in. Starting the car first and warming it up would certainly make the ride better. She squinted and looked closer at the windshield. There might be little enough snow that she could use the wipers to clear it off and not have to go back outside.

Olympia turned the key in the ignition, and bless its dependable little German cylinders, it started right up. It was only when she flicked the wiper switch and nothing happened that she began to worry. She could hear the wiper motor grinding away, but nothing was moving. Olympia slid back out of the car, went around to the front and brushed away the snow where the wipers should be, but there was nothing. They were gone, snapped off at the base. Olympia Brown was going nowhere, and the snow was falling faster and faster.

In Brookfield Frederick and Jim were constructing lunch. Frederick was of the quick and convenient school of gastronomy and suggested heating up a can of soup. Jim was not and offered to make omelets with assorted leftovers, garnished with three cheeses and black olives. In the end Jim won out, and the two were sitting down to a lovely lunch with thimblefuls of leftover wine beside each warmed plate as the storm kicked up in earnest. But despite the delicious lunch before them, the two men were worried about Olympia. She should have been home by now, and neither of them wanted to think of her being out on the roads.

Jim put the makings of a third omelet in the fridge for when she got in, and Frederick kept looking at his watch and going to the kitchen door. Even the cats were restless, but then they always were when a storm was brewing. Frederick wanted to call Olympia on her cell phone, but Jim wisely counseled that distracting her on the road would do no good at all. Frederick woefully agreed.

There was a dark discomfort in the Watkins-Brown homestead, and Miss Winslow, irregularly bing-bonging from her spot on the mantel in the sitting room, only made it worse.

Outside the church Olympia's initial panic subsided almost as quickly as it had come on, and she switched into survival mode. Think and be sensible, woman, you were bred for this. She grabbed the emergency blanket and the box of granola bars out of the car and slipped and slid around the building, where she let herself back into the office. There was no way she could get her car fixed, and even if she could, fifteen minutes in the parking lot had been enough to convince her to shelter in place. Even if they lost power, she had her winter clothing, the extra blanket and her cell phone, and she could even make a bed out of the pew cushions, if she needed to.

When her breathing and body temperature returned to normal, she picked up the phone and called home. An anxious Frederick picked up.

"Where are you?"

"Relax darling, I'm safe and warm, at least for now, while we still have power. I can't use the car. Someone has sabotaged my windshield wipers, and I can't drive it."

"What are you talking about? Do you want us to come down and get you?" She could hear his voice getting higher and higher.

"Not on your life—or mine, for that matter. No, I'm afraid my dear little Emily has had another episode, and this time she's taken it out on my van. I'm locked in, I'm safe, and the roads are god-awful. Even if I could drive the van, I wouldn't dare. It's really bad out there, and it's only just started. Nope, I'm staying put."

"I don't like the idea of you being alone in a storm like this."

"I don't much like it either, but it beats the hell out of being alone and stuck on the road somewhere, don't you agree?"

"You have a point, Olympia, but let's check in with each other from time to time. That way I won't be worrying myself silly."

Olympia smiled. "Goes both ways, my love. I'll be thinking about you and Jim, you know."

Even over the sound of the wind outside, she could hear the exasperation in his voice.

"Jim and I have heat, candles, a battery radio, food and cats. You have an emergency blanket, a box of granola bars and a nut case prowling around."

"She's gone home. I'm in a nice, big old church. I have heat and hot water, working toilets, a gas stove, power and a phone, two of them actually. I'll be fine. I've even got a Bible to read, and if there's one thing a church has in abundance, its candles."

"Will you do me one courtesy and call the police and let them know you are there alone?"

"If it will make you feel better, of course I will, and actually, I think it's a good idea."

"I don't like this, Olympia."

"Neither do I, darling, but considering the circumstances, I don't have much of a choice. I'll survive."

"Call me in an hour."

"Promise."

Olympia pocketed the phone and set about making a nest for herself. There was a fireplace in the office, but God only knew if it still worked, so that was out of the question. She turned the heat back up and set off in search of some creature comforts. There was an electric kettle in the kitchen and certainly some assorted things to eat. She looked around. A pitcher of water? Yes. Teabags? Yes. Instant coffee? Perish the thought! Olympia Brown had once vowed she'd never be desperate enough to drink that. Yes to the oyster crackers and, lo and behold, a few things in the food pantry donation basket, if she got desperate. She was home free. She'd go back to the office and settle these things in, call the police and alert them to the fact she was there, and then, after something to eat and drink, she'd go into the sanctuary and drag in some pew cushions. Frederick would say, "she lacked for nothing she'd got," and he'd be right. She smiled … dear Frederick.

Outside the light was fading, and inside the lights were beginning to flicker. It was already gloomy because of the clouds overhead, but now it was getting truly dark. It was time to go and get what would become her bed while she could still see.

Outside the warm and brightly lit office the rest of the building was already cold as charity, another Frederick phrase. It really was a barn of a place, but a beautiful and lovingly maintained barn. As she made her way to the short corridor leading to the sanctuary, she could hear the sounds of organ music. It made her smile. Well, I'm not alone then, am I? she thought. I've got old Jeremy for company. I wonder what's he's up to on a day like this?

When she entered the sanctuary, the music stopped. In the chill, vaulted silence she pulled two of the nearest dusty rose pew cushions off the benches and dragged them out the door, across the parish hall and into her office. Like everything else in the place, they were cold to the touch and would need some time in the heat to warm up before she could use them. Must call the police, she told herself as she went out toward the kitchen for a cup, some water and some cutlery, and I will, right after I get myself settled.

Twenty-Seven

Back in her office, Olympia looked around for the least drafty place to put the pew cushions and spotted several small puddles of water on the floor. A leak? A spill? She looked more closely at the shape. They were melted footprints, several of them, and they weren't hers.

While she'd been in the sanctuary, someone must have come in. There was no doubt in her mind who, but had Emily come in and left again, or was she still in the church somewhere, waiting to make another surprise appearance?

Olympia could no longer tell from the water on the floor, but maybe there were still some footprints to be seen in the snow outside the door. Would there be one set or two? If there were two, Emily had gone back out. If there was only one, she was still in the church.

Before she went to the window to look, she locked her inside office door, a heavy oak Victorian monstrosity undoubtedly added during one of the many expansions to the place over the years. Olympia was not interested in its provenance, but she was profoundly grateful for its massive thickness as the lock thunked soundly into place.

Looking through the window, she could see indentations of footprints, but they were already disappearing, and there was no way to tell whether they were coming or going. Olympia returned to her desk and picked up the phone. It was time to call the police. Not knowing the number off the top of her head, she dialed 9-1-1.

"I know this sounds far-fetched, Officer, but I'm the current minister of the Salt Rock Fellowship, and I'm stranded in the chapel. I have every reason to believe there's a woman in here with me who may want to do me harm. I need someone to come and get me. I'll sleep in a jail cell, if I have to, but I need to get out of here." She kept her voice low so if Emily was within earshot, she couldn't overhear what Olympia was saying or who she was talking to.

"Why do you think that person wants to hurt you?" asked the officer who'd answered the phone.

"Because the same person just broke the windshield wipers on my car so I couldn't leave if I wanted to, which I don't, because of the weather. I've locked myself in my office, but the woman has a key to the outside door."

"How do you know it's a woman?"

Olympia knew if she screamed all the things she wanted to at that particular moment, she would seriously compromise any chance she might have of getting help.

"Because she's been stalking me, she disabled my car, and she threatened me less than an hour ago."

"But you're safe for now?"

"More or less. I'm locked in my office, and I still have power, and my cell phone is working, but who knows how long that will last? I've got blankets and warm clothes and water, but she's somewhere in here or out there, and she's out to get me."

"You're sure of that?"

Olympia growled under her breath and said. "Yes, Officer, I am, and to be honest, I'm frightened."

"Okay, Reverend. We'll do the best we can, but you understand that we have to give priority to highway and medical emergencies. We'll send someone as soon as possible, but in this weather we can't make any promises. Can you lock the outside door from the inside?"

With the phone still clamped to her ear, Olympia walked over to the door. There was no inside lock. "No, I can't double lock it, if that's what you mean."

"Can you push something heavy against it?"

"I suppose."

"Well, do it now, and then sit tight and wait for us to get there. We'll do the best we can."

"Thank you, Officer."

First things first: barricade the door. It took some doing, but with brute force and several un-clerical curses, she managed to push, drag and heave the big claw-foot mahogany desk into position. Now what, she asked herself? If she weren't so nervous about Emily's intentions and whereabouts, this could have been an adventure she might have enjoyed telling her grandchildren, but such was not the case.

Next on her mental to-do list was calling Frederick. Should she tell him about Emily and scare him out of his socks so he might risk his neck trying to get down there? The obvious answer was, no way. Before she could make the call, the lights flickered more dramatically and then went out for good. "Double damnation," she hissed and began feeling around in the half-light for the candles and the matches she'd left on the desk that was now wedged against the door. She remembered that her cell phone had a flashlight and successfully used it to locate the candles and get one lighted.

Olympia called Frederick on her cell phone and assured him that even though they'd lost power, she was fine and she had indeed asked the police to come and get her.

"You're sure you're okay? Your voice sounds strained." Frederick was no fool.

"I'm fine. Anyone would be nervous in this kind of storm. That's all it is."

"Well, give me your number there, and I'll call you the next time."

"No, stick with the cell phone, it's almost fully charged."

When she disconnected, she could hear the building creaking and groaning in the wind. Was it the wind, or was it someone moving outside her door? Keep calm. God Herself couldn't get through that door if she wanted to. Even though she'd made it, the little joke was lost on Olympia. She wanted this nightmare to be over, but there were still several hours to get through before it would be. Even then, how would it end?

On the other side of the double-locked, oak-paneled door, Emily was sitting in the church administrator's chair, counting the minutes. It was getting colder and colder, but she'd made it this far, and she was not going to back away now. She could hear Olympia's voice inside the office, but she couldn't make out the words. No matter. Even if she did try and call for help, no one was coming out in this. Time and the beautiful, terrible storm were on her side. She pulled her down coat tighter around her shoulders and pushed the collar up around her ears. In a few minutes she would knock on the door and give Olympia one more chance.

In Brookfield Jim and Frederick had something in addition to Olympia to worry about. Cadeau, the green-eyed black cat, was missing. Neither of them remembered letting him out, but they had been going in and out of the main house, getting wood and securing the future office against the storm. By mutual agreement they decided not to tell Olympia the next time she called. She had enough on her mind without adding to it. The two men searched everywhere they could think of, calling, cajoling, shaking the treat can, even muttering a few curses—sotto voce, of course—but no cat.

Neither of them would admit to fearing the worst, but as the sound and fury of the storm increased, so did their concern. None of this was in any way helped by Miss Winslow's clock having a mini-tantrum of its own, bing-ing and boing-ing with increasing frequency.

"I'm going to check on Olympia," said Frederick, but when he tried her cell phone number, it wouldn't connect.

"Try the church number," suggested Jim.

"Jesus," spat Frederick, "I'm getting the busy circuit message, what else? I don't need this for one goddamn minute."

"Give me the phone, and I'll try the police down there. I do believe you said she was going to call them, did you not?"

Frederick nodded miserably, no longer trying to hide his agitation.

When Jim got through to the police, he learned that the lines were already down, but before the power had gone out they'd had a call from a minister named Olympia Brown, asking for assistance.

"Is that all?" said Frederick. "They've had a phone call, wonderful. Do they plan to do anything, or are they going to wait for spring?"

Jim was feeling every bit as frantic as Frederick, but with the skills honed in his years of priesthood, he pushed down his own concern in order to help his friend.

"They made sure she was safely sheltered and told her they would get to her as soon as they could. She's safe and out of the storm, Frederick, and she's nobody's fool. She might be cold, but she's not injured and does know how to take care of herself."

"Of course you're right, Jim. It's just that I feel so bloody helpless, that's all."

"So do I, my friend. Believe me, so do I."

Emily was so cold now that she had to keep moving to stay warm. She was circling around the outside office with her mittened fingers clamped around her flashlight. Finally, she stopped and knocked at the door that separated her from Olympia, three sharp raps. Then she called out, "Reverend Olympia? Open the door. This is all wrong. It's freezing out here, please let me in. We need to talk."

On the other side of the door, Olympia Brown was torn between compassion and self-preservation. Emily was ill and needed help, but was she capable of handling an obsessed and possibly dangerous woman by herself? Should she try? What would happen to both of them if she didn't? Could she live with herself if she didn't at least make an effort? And where the hell were the police? It had been almost two hours since she'd called them. As if in response, another blast of wind screeched through the trees and slammed against the northeast wall of the building.

Against her better judgment—and really, is there such a thing as better judgment in a situation like this?—Olympia stood on the other side of the door and released the inside lock. With her food wedged against the back of the door, and staying well out of sight, she eased it open just far enough to see the glow from Emily's flashlight on the other side.

"Emily, we're here by ourselves in a dangerous storm. We don't have light or heat, and it's only getting colder. It would be better for both of us if we could help each other instead of talking through a door, not knowing what the other is thinking of doing."

In response Emily whimpered, "I'm sorry I broke your windshield wipers. I wanted to keep you here so I could have time alone with you. Now we're both going to freeze to death. I'm sorry."

Olympia spoke softly through the space between them. "If I open the door, do I have your word that you'll stay calm, and we can work as a team, like we did last Saturday night with the kids? You were terrific. We need to help each other to stay warm until the power comes back on or someone can get through to get us out. Can we do this together, Emily? Can you do this with me?"

"Uh huh."

"Is that a yes?"

"Yes, Reverend," she whispered.

Olympia held her breath, stepped back and slowly opened the door, and Emily, red-faced and shaking, stepped into the candlelit room. She stood staring at the floor like a shamed child while Olympia closed the door behind her in order to preserve what residual heat remained.

"Why is the desk over there?" Emily pointed at the outside door.

"I was trying to clear a place on the floor to put these pew cushions." Olympia didn't like lying, but considering the circumstances she didn't give it a second thought. "I figured since I would be spending the night here, I might as well make myself comfortable. Besides, hard as they are, they'll be better than the lying on the floor. Warmer, too." She pointed to the visitor chair. "Pull that closer, and I'll light another candle. We can at least warm our hands—and I think there might be some old altar drapes in the sanctuary. If we get really cold, we can wrap those around our legs and feet."

"Do you want me to go get them?" Emily was now crumpled into her chair with her hands clenched on her knees.

At that moment, Olympia could feel nothing but pity for the poor woman. Mental illness was not like a cold. You can't take a few aspirin, drink lots of water and have it go away in a week. This was a constant and debilitating companion. It was part of who she was.

"No, stay here and warm yourself up a little, and then we'll see what we need. Whoever expected the storm to be this bad? I don't think I've ever seen anything like this."

"I was just a baby when the famous blizzard of 1978 came through. I remember my parents talking about it."

Now was not the time to mention that Emily once told her she'd been raised in a foster home.

Twenty-Eight

"Tell me about your parents, Emily." Olympia wanted to keep her talking. She knew it would help to ease the tension, but more than that, for some reason, dead silence felt so much colder and more threatening than conversation.

"My parents died a couple of years ago. It was a murder-suicide. I found them. My father had Alzheimer's. He was so bad my mother couldn't take care of him anymore. I could have helped, but she never asked me. He had an old army gun. She killed him, then lay down beside him and killed herself."

"I'm so sorry," whispered Olympia. "That must have been awful for you."

"I've always had … problems. They didn't like to talk about it, but I could do more for myself than they ever let me. That's why I moved out. I had to show them I could take care of myself, but then I didn't know what was happening at home."

She shook her head as the tears rolled down her cheeks. "I could have helped, and they wouldn't let me." Her voice was barely above a whisper as she continued.

"That's why it was so wonderful when you asked me to help you last Saturday night. Nobody asks me to help do anything, so that's when I really knew you cared for me."

"Caring for someone is different than being in love with them, Emily."

"Don't say that. I don't want to hear you say that." Her voice began to rise.

"Take a deep breath, and hear me out. I think it's important to find out what we do best and then find ways of doing it. Don't you agree?"

Emily nodded and said nothing, but she was no longer twisting her fingers.

"Well, that's what I hope we can talk about tonight. But before we say any more, and before it gets any colder in here, I need to go to the bathroom. Then I'll see if I can find something in the sanctuary we can wrap up in. And you … you take your flashlight and go out into the kitchen and see if you can find any of those great big tablecloths the ladies use on Sundays. We need layers. Isn't that what the survival manuals tell you, to dress in layers? Okay, I think we have a plan."

Olympia hoped her cheery, positive words would carry them over the few minutes without incident. She really needed to go to the toilet, and she didn't want to leave Emily alone with lighted candles or in a position where she could turn the tables and lock Olympia out of her own office. "Come on, then, the sooner we get moving, the sooner we can get back in here where it's at least four or five degrees warmer than in the rest of the place."

At first Emily moved as though she was drugged. Her steps were slow and uncertain, but then she straightened up and began walking toward the kitchen. Olympia moved as quickly as she could without letting the candle go out. She cupped it with her hand and quick-stepped toward the bathroom via the main door of the church, where she threw back the deadbolt and unlocked the door. If the police were able to get there, she wanted to make damn sure they could get in.

After a very fast and focused pee, she checked in the kitchen, where Emily was still opening and closing drawers in search of table linens. Good.

"I'll be back in two secs," she called over her shoulder. Still cupping the candle, she went back out into the sanctuary. It was dim and frightening, but Olympia was on a mission. She went to the back of the church proper, climbed the stairs to the organ loft and secured the candle so she could use both hands. She remembered seeing a pile of old velvet drapes among the detritus that always collects in unused corners of churches. Boxes of Christmas decorations, half-burned altar candles—grab some of those, Olympia—piles of music and, rumpled in a corner, a great red velvet hanging. It exhaled clouds of dust as she pulled it out and shook it over the balcony rail, but it would more than do the trick. For one insane moment, she felt like Scarlett O'Hara in *Gone with the Wind.* She held it up and squinted at it. It was huge. She could rip it in half, if she had to. That way she wouldn't have to sit under it next to Emily, which was probably a good idea.

Clutching the candle with one hand and dragging the velvet drape with the other, she returned to her office. There she found Emily sitting in a chair with two long, heavy linen tablecloths folded in her lap.

"Good going, Emily. I've got more candles and this." She held up a corner of the drape. "Here, you hold on to one end and help me straighten it out."

"I'll do that," said Emily. "That way you can light some more of those candles. They don't really throw much heat, but it's better than nothing. If my hands are warm, then the rest of me feels better."

Olympia couldn't argue with that. Between them, they managed to get four of the altar candles tied together so they wouldn't tip over, and Olympia wedged them between the heaviest books she could find. Then the two women wrapped themselves in everything they could find and settled in for the long haul, or until they fell asleep, or, please God, someone wearing a dark blue uniform showed up in a vehicle with four-wheel drive and a working heater.

Olympia didn't make a habit of praying for specific things, but on that night she made an exception. She peeked at her watch. It was just past seven. It was going to be a long, cold night, but all in all, she supposed it could have been worse. Careful, she thought. Her mother always used to say, "Be careful what you wish for." Cancel that, she re-thought, and burrowed deeper into her layers, where it was almost warm.

The power in Brookfield went out just after seven, and for a few disjointed moments, Frederick tried to convince Jim they should go out and try to reach Olympia. Jim countered with a stern talking to and a rather large brandy, which eventually made Frederick see the futility of such a gambit. Two hours later, the clock finally shut up, and the two were sitting by the fire playing Scrabble by candlelight and arguing about spelling. Frederick, of course, used the English spelling, and Jim, of course, did not; but it more or less kept their minds off the health and safety of their beloved Olympia and the cat. It was going to be a long night, but at least they had each other to worry with.

When Olympia woke up, she was completely disoriented. Her first thought was disbelief that she'd actually fallen asleep. The second thought was the candles, which were shorter but still flickering, and Emily, who was gone. Olympia threw off her layers and struggled to her feet. She was cold and felt stiff all over. She looked around the room.

Everything was in place, the office door was closed, but Emily, with her flashlight and everything in which she was wrapped, had vanished.

"Damn," muttered Olympia. The woman was mentally ill. She could freeze to death, and with all the nooks and crannies in this old place, she could be anywhere. What the hell had happened? That's when she noticed something flickering— no, flashing—in the whirling snow outside the window. Sweet Jesus, the police had finally arrived. She looked at her watch. It was almost nine. How long had she been asleep? How long had Emily been gone?

Olympia literally ran to the main front door and yanked it open to two uniformed, well-muffled police officers and an icy blast of wind-driven snow.

"Officers Bill McGrath and Elizabeth Wainright, Upper Cape PD. Are you Reverend Brown?"

Olympia nodded in relief. "Thank God you're here. Come in. We have to find Emily, the woman that is, or was, here with me, but she's gone missing. She's the woman I told you about when I called for help."

"What are you talking about, Ma'am?"

"Come inside, and I'll explain."

The officers followed Olympia into her office, where the temperature was still marginally above freezing and, despite the surreal circumstances to the contrary, the altar candles cast a welcoming glow.

Where to begin, thought Olympia?

"I called you for help for two reasons. The obvious one is that I'm stranded in this place without heat, but there is a woman here with me who is mentally ill. She's threatened me and disabled my car. I was able to calm her down and get her into the office and keep her talking, but I must have done my job too well, because I think we both fell asleep. When I woke up just before you got here, she was gone. I can't believe she's so distraught she'd go outside in this, but she's unpredictable. We can't leave until we find her."

"Where do you think she might be?"

"This is an old building. There are walls behind walls, false doors, and there's even supposed to be a secret room somewhere. She knows the place better than I do, but I guess we just keep looking until we find her."

"And if we don't?"

Olympia grimaced and shook her head. "I don't know."

"Do you think she might have a weapon of some kind?" said Officer McGrath.

The image of the gun that had killed her parents flashed through Olympia's mind, but she pushed it away.

"I don't think so."

"Do you think she might harm herself?"

"Like I said, she's unpredictable. I thought I'd talked her down, and she'd be okay until help arrived, but I was wrong."

"Look, why don't you go sit in the police van and warm up while we look for her?"

"Thanks, but no thanks. I know the building better than you do. This place is over two hundred years old. There are cupboards and closets everywhere. I'll be warm if I keep moving, but before we move one inch, I'm going to blow out these candles. I may be freezing, but setting the church on fire is not going to help anyone."

The house in Brookfield was getting colder and colder. Frederick was beginning to worry about the pipes freezing, but there was nothing he could do. The only room in the house that was warm was the sitting room. Jim and Frederick were amply supplied with candles, firewood and things to read. They had tuned the battery-operated radio to a classical music station, and that, along with the hiss and crackle of the fire, made it all look and sound almost normal. But it wasn't, and they both knew it. Olympia Brown, beloved by them both, and a little black mischief maker named Cadeau were not with them, and there wasn't a thing either of them could do about it. By unspoken agreement, each tried not to worry the other about the very real and present dangers facing the lady and the cat.

Twenty-Nine

Olympia was beginning to regret declining the offer to sit in the police cruiser and get warm. She could not remember ever being so cold, and if she was beginning to suffer with it, then where was poor Emily, and how cold was she?

They'd been all over the upstairs social area and kitchen and were now downstairs calling her name and working their way through the Sunday School rooms and the children's chapel. They'd left the sanctuary for last, because it was going to be the biggest and the coldest. Logically, a person trying to hide in this cold would go to a warm, snug space. But was there any logic in trying to out-think Emily? Probably not, thought Olympia, but that didn't stop them from soldiering on.

The unspoken fear was that she'd gone outside and was lost somewhere in the storm, but they had to exhaust all possibilities inside first. Where could she be?

"What the hell? Oops, excuse me, Reverend."

"What? Did you find something, Officer?"

"Please call me Liz. I hear something. It sounds like organ music. Listen! There it goes again. Who in God's name would be playing the organ at this hour of the night in the freezing cold in the middle of a blizzard?"

I know just who, thought Olympia, because she could hear it, too; but she was far too cold to try and explain it. Besides, who would believe her?

Through chattering teeth she said, "It's the wind. It does that sometimes, but it makes me think we might find Emily in the sanctuary. Come on."

Olympia led the charge up the stairs, through the narrow foyer and into the great empty space. Because of the pale light reflected off the snow and the two-story, clear glass windows, it wasn't dark but rather an eerie grey. It was easy to make out the shapes of the pews and where the aisles were located. The three went down to the front, fanned out and slowly worked their way, row by row, to the back. Nothing. Where was she?

"What's up there?" Officer McGrath pointed up to the balcony at the back of the church.

"It's the organ loft. I suppose the choir used it in the old days. I was up there earlier this evening. Mostly it's the instrument itself and a lot of seasonal storage—spell that junk. I didn't see any hiding places up there, but then I wasn't looking."

"I'll go up," said Officer Liz. "I probably haven't had enough exercise today."

They were all too cold and tired to laugh.

"I'll go with you," said Olympia. "If she is up there she might feel less threatened by me."

When they reached the top of the stairs, Olympia could swear it was not as cold up there. Of course, heat rises, but there was no heat to rise. So why was it warmer? It was also much darker. Liz Wainright switched on her flashlight and started looking into the space between the bench and the pedals. Nothing. Then she moved around to the right to see if there was any place behind the instrument into which someone could possibly fit.

"Don't touch me!" screeched Emily.

She was squeezed in between the wind-chest and the pipe cabinet.

"Let me talk to her," whispered Olympia, quietly moving around to where Emily could see her.

"Emily, you can come out now. I'm here, and I'll keep you safe, I promise. No one is going to hurt you."

"You hate me."

"I don't hate you, I want to help you. It's cold, and it's late. You must be exhausted. Come with me, and we can go get warm."

"Get away from me."

"I'm not coming near you, Emily. You have to come to me. Come on, now, one step at a time."

She could hear Officer Wainright breathing behind her, and she could see her own breath in the beam of the flashlight. "Come out Emily, please."

Emily slowly began to inch forward. It was not going to be easy for her to get out of there, but Olympia didn't dare move.

"Keep coming, Emily. That's good, you're almost there. Come on," Olympia slowly lifted her hand toward the terrified woman. "One more step, that's right. Now take my hand."

When she could finally move freely, Emily ignored the outstretched hand and moved like an unwound mechanical doll to where Officer McGrath was standing at the edge of the balcony. She stopped just out of his reach and stood looking at him. Then without a word of warning, she turned away and dropped headfirst over the railing.

The two women raced down the stairs to find McGrath and Emily Goodale in a tangled, moaning heap. Olympia and Liz assessed the situation and then called for an ambulance.

Later, back in the station house, he would tell them he didn't know how he'd known, but standing there, looking up toward balcony, there had been no question in his mind but that she was going over. The good news was, when Emily jumped, he was standing close enough to be able to lunge forward and break her fall. The bad news was that in so doing, he'd broken his collarbone. Emily fared a little worse with a broken right arm and fractured left leg.

There was no way anyone would be getting to a hospital in the immediate future. McGrath was in pain but would be helped by immobilizing his arm and shoulder. They did this by binding him with one of the church tablecloths. Emily was a different story. She was in severe physical pain, but because of it, she wasn't trying to escape or cause further damage to herself. Closer examination would later reveal that she'd suffered a compound fracture of her forearm when she hit the back of a pew.

Using more pew cushions and the velvet altar drape that Olympia dragged back from her office, they made Emily as physically comfortable as they could. Outside the storm was at its height, and exhausted road crews were doing the best they could, but the storm was too much for anyone. The only way they'd get to Cape Cod hospital in Hyannis would be to follow directly behind a plow. After the better part of a very cold hour a gigantic, multi-wheeled plow, followed by a brightly flashing ambulance, arrived on the scene. Olympia didn't know whether to laugh, cry or jump for joy, so she sang out a most Handelian, high soprano "Alleluia," and made ready to vacate the premises.

Before leaving, Olympia made a quick dash back to the office for her personal things and the church directory. She suggested that she sit in the ambulance with Emily in the belief that her presence might provide some measure of emotional comfort. The ride itself consisted of over an hour of crawling through what looked like a white cotton wind tunnel, but eventually they made it. Once there and unloaded,

Olympia was more than grateful to let the professionals take over. By then it was two in the morning, and she needed to find a phone that worked so she could call home. After that she would see about finding a place to sleep.

When the phone rang, Frederick lunged for the one in the sitting room and Jim ran out to the kitchen to pick up the extension.

"I'm okay. I'm not hurt, and I'm not cold."

"Where the hell are you?" roared Frederick.

"I'm at the Cape Cod Hospital with an injured parishioner and a less injured police officer. I'll tell you everything when I get home, which may take a while. I'll spend the night here on the Cape somewhere, and when the roads are passable, you can come down and get me."

"You're sure you're all right?" said Jim.

"Really, I am, honest."

"But somebody's been hurt."

"I said it was a long story, but we all survived. The police were able to get us to a place of warmth and safety. If I weren't so wired I'd ask for a cup of coffee, but even I'm not that stupid. Go to bed, both of you. I'll either spend the night at the hospital or in a nearby motel. I'm fine."

By mutual agreement, neither Jim nor Frederick mentioned the missing cat. Olympia had enough to deal with without adding Cadeau to her list of concerns. By now even Thunderfoot, the old yellow tom, was nosing around, looking for him.

"And so to bed," said Frederick with a huge and noisy yawn.

"*Pax vobiscum,*" answered Jim.

"Meoooowl," said Cadeau.

"Bloody hell!"

The two men turned as one to watch Cadeau yawn and stretch and then saunter out of the bedroom and toward the kitchen and his food dish.

"Meoooooooooooowl!" he repeated for emphasis

Thirty

Olympia spent what was left of the night in a spare bed in the hospital. Because of the suicide attempt, Emily was treated for the broken bones and then admitted. She would be kept there or at another facility for a period of observation and evaluation. Officer Bill McGrath was treated and released and, like Olympia, stayed at the hospital until the roads were clear enough for him to be taken home. Outside, the storm continued whirling mass devastation and destruction in all directions, and the birds and the beasties and the humans wisely kept out of its way.

When Olympia awoke and crawled out of bed, it was just after eight and still snowing. She pulled back the window curtain to see almost two feet of snow. The actual depths varied widely because of the high winds. In some places drifts were five and six feet high, and in contrast to that, whole expanses of fields and parking lots were swept almost clean by the unrelenting winds. Plows and road crews were still working nonstop, but the end was in sight. One of the nurses told her the snow should start to taper off in the late morning, and the sun might even make it out before it was due to set that evening.

By late afternoon a dramatic fuchsia and orange sunset became visible over the undulating, snowy landscape. In its rosy afterglow Olympia staggered out of Jim's car. Sometime during their absence the power had been restored, and no one was more appreciative than the lady of the house. She wanted nothing more than to have a hot bath, crawl into bed and sleep like the dead until further notice. Jim set about making tea. They knew the tale would be interesting, but by the look of the weary reverend, it would be some time in coming.

"We've got some pasta and some vegetables," said Frederick. "I'm sure we can do something with that."

"Leave it to me, my friend. I don't think herself is going to want anything right now, but I'll set some aside for her. All I need is some garlic and olive oil, and I can arrange to have a pasta primavera on the table in twenty-five minutes from the time you say go."

"Wine first," said Frederick.

"Wine not?" said Jim.

Both cats glared at the good Father, lifted their tails and exited the kitchen.

The next morning, even though Frederick assured her he liked the old one just fine, Olympia felt like a new woman. The sun was shining, the blue-white of the snow was blindingly beautiful, and the three of them had nothing to do but kick back, feed the fire and themselves at regular intervals, and enjoy it. Well, almost nothing. Olympia had some unfinished church business.

After her second cup of coffee she went back to her office corner of their bedroom to tie off the last of the loose ends of the Emily saga so that she could fully enjoy the gift of time that two feet of snow and mostly impassable roads will give you. The first call was to Phil Rutledge, the regular minister of Salt Rock. She filled him in on all the details of what had happened with Emily and where she was being cared for. She assured him she'd call Catherine, the Board President and Thom Whitehead. As well as updating them on Emily, she'd make sure they were able to take care of the building post-storm and pre-Sunday.

Rutledge's response was understandably mixed. He was relieved that the incident had been so well handled but slightly uncomfortable that it had all happened when he was out of town. Olympia did her best to reassure him.

"If you think about it, Phil, it probably wouldn't have happened on your shift. I'm convinced my coming here was the catalyst. I was different. You knew her, and she knew you. I had no history with her. She started dropping in on me and following me around almost from the day I started. It was only after the Valentine's Day cook-off with the kids that things went really bad. Before that point it was sad and annoying, but then it got scary. Now that it's all said and done, I don't think we could have asked for a better outcome. It's true she's hurt, but she's in a safe place where she will be cared for and treated. If Officer McGrath hadn't been where he was and hadn't moved as quickly as he did, she could have killed herself. That would have been a real mess."

"That does rather put it into perspective, Olympia, thank you."

"Enjoy the rest of your sabbatical, Phil. It should be clear sailing down here from now on."

"Ministers shouldn't count their chickens before they're christened, Olympia."

"Don't tell anyone, Phil, but I failed chicken counting in seminary. I kept getting them mixed up with the turkeys."

At that he laughed. "Take care of the church, Olympia. They're lucky to have you, and so am I."

"Will do," she said. "It's an honor and a privilege to help a colleague."

Next on the call list was Catherine Allen, who would communicate with the rest of the Board, and after that, she was home free—literally. It had been a very long forty-eight hours, and she was feeling every nanosecond of it, but

Olympia Brown was officially off the clock. If somebody asked, she would tell them even her hair was tired. It was too early to have a glass of wine, so maybe some fresh coffee and something with sugar in it would wake her up and tide her over.

When she returned to the sitting room, Frederick and Jim looked up from their respective books.

"Well?" Said Frederick.

"Well what?"

"Are you going to give us the intimate and gory details of your adventure, or do we have to play twenty questions?"

Olympia dropped into her chair and was immediately set upon by both cats. When the three of them were settled, she began the story with the broken rose and Emily's unannounced visit just as the storm was starting. She ended it with the two of them in the back of an ambulance, skidding toward the hospital.

"That's one for the books, Olympia," said Jim, shaking his head.

"And you have written the final chapter on this one, my love." Frederick was shaking an index finger at her. "Book closed."

"For now anyway."

He looked at her aghast. "What in hell are you talking about? Miss crazy-legs is safely stowed away in hospital, the church didn't blow over, and the powers that be will hold down the fort until the end of the week. I repeat, what the hell are you talking about?"

Olympia sighed, and the cats wiggled and resettled themselves. "Things like this are never cut and dried. Emily, whatever she is or isn't, is a member of the church, and I don't think she has any immediate family."

"Your point is?" said Jim. There was an edge in his voice. Even saintly Jim could get annoyed with Olympia's unending earth-mothering.

"I mean, we can't just chuck her out of the church because she's had an episode. She's mentally ill, and she needs care and understanding."

"Olympia! The woman sabotaged your van, she lied about you, and who knows what else she had in mind with that dead rose thing. She was hiding in the church, and she either got too cold to carry out her intentions, or she changed her mind. Would you please get out of your goody-two-shoes? The woman did not have warm and fuzzy thoughts for you. She intended to harm you."

"But she didn't."

Frederick was flushed, and his voice was rising.

"Frederick has a point, Olympia. You often don't see the evil lurking in the hearts of men or women, and we both love you for it, but it's not always a good thing."

Jim, bless him, had diverted the oncoming domestic storm with firm and gentle reason. Olympia sheepishly got off her high-horse.

"Will you actually be able to learn anything about Emily, considering you are not family?" asked Jim.

"I'm not sure. When I go and visit her, I can ask. Maybe because I'm her minister, they might tell me." Olympia held up her hand to ward off their protests. "And before you both start in on me again, why shouldn't I visit her in the hospital? She can't attack me there. She might not even want to see me, but I feel I should make the effort. She's ill, she's not evil."

Olympia had made her point but was saved a triumphant harrumph from Frederick by the sound of the telephone. It was her daughter, calling to see how they'd all fared during the storm.

"Is it really as bad as it looks on TV?" she asked.

"Yes, and then some. I got stranded in the church and had to be rescued by the police, so I've got some stories to tell."

"I'll bet, and I can't wait to hear them," said her daughter.

Don't hold your breath, thought Olympia. "So when are you all coming east?"

"I'm thinking about May or June. Will you be around?"

"My darling woman, if you are planning to visit, I'll be here. Make no mistake about that."

Olympia could swear she could hear her daughter smiling. "I'm finished with the Salt Rock appointment in mid-April, so anything after that. We've got the room, and I hope that by then I'll even have my own office to serve as a second guest room, if needed. Just say the word."

When she hung up the phone, Olympia realized she was beginning to feel more like herself and less like a wrung-out dishrag. The men had a point, but so did she. She would be careful, cautious even; but for her own sake and for Emily's, she needed to learn the truth behind the fiction. Which, if any, of Emily's multiple stories were true? Was she an orphan? Were her parents really dead, and if so, how and when did they die? A visit to the hospital might clarify some of that. Phil Rutledge might be able to help. Then it came to her. It was so simple these days. She could check Emily out on Facebook and social media in general and see if she could find any references to her parents or their deaths on good old Google.

Now that Olympia had a plan, the rest of the day was hers to design. Today she would enjoy one of the books she'd been promising herself to read, knit that other sock and spend some extra time with Miss Winslow's diary. But first …

"Say, Jim?"

"Mmm?"

"What kind of wine would go best with a peanut butter and Marshmallow Fluff sandwich?"

Jim never missed a beat. "Kool-Aid," he snorted.

April 1, 1863

It is the first day of April, and while I have no wish to play the fool, my heart is lighter. I believe the spring has finally come to stay. This house is not a house of mourning but one of fond memories. I think of Jonathan's father Jared and my Aunt Louisa. I think of my mother, long gone now (I can no longer recall her face.), and my father, somewhat more recently. I do have a daguerreotype image of him. The memories are good, and they comfort me as I think of the days and the road ahead.

More Anon, LFW

Thirty-One

The next day, everyone in their immediate vicinity was still snowbound and luxuriating in a second day off. Olympia, Frederick and Jim each had a plan which did not involve going outside for any reason other than to get more wood, fill the bird feeders or make snow angels.

With her power and internet restored, Olympia ensconced herself at her computer with the intention of trying to find some answers to the questions she'd put to herself the day before. While she was doing that, Jim and Frederick planned to put some muscle into the office/studio/guest room project. The cats aligned themselves back-to-back on the mat in front of the woodstove, and all was right with the world. It was a *Saturday Evening Post* cover image of domestic simplicity and comfort. At least, that was the plan.

In her corner office in the bedroom, Olympia picked up the phone and called Phil Rutledge.

"Hi Phil, its Olympia. Do you have a couple of minutes?"

He did.

"Can you tell me what you know about Emily Goodale's background? She told me one story when I first met her, Charlotte had a different one, and then Emily gave me a whole new story the night we were trapped in the storm."

"What has she told you?" asked Phil.

"First she said she was raised in a foster home in North Adams, and she currently works in a nursing home. The night of the storm, she told me that her parents died in a murder-suicide. Charlotte said she worked in a local restaurant, the Cape Something-or-other.'

"The Crepe-Codder."

"That's the one."

Phil continued. "The murder suicide is true. It happened about five years ago. Her mother had Alzheimer's, and word was that her dad couldn't take the strain any longer."

"Was that in question?" asked Olympia.

"Hard to say. Nothing was ever proven. There was no note, and everybody knew how bad it was for the old man, so I don't think anybody really challenged it. Emily was a wreck and had to be hospitalized for a time."

"Does she have any family or anyone else to advocate for her?"

"Not that I know of. I suppose that's something I'd better look into when I get back," said Phil.

"Well, she's going to be in the hospital for a while, but when she gets out, she'll need something."

"You've done more than your share, Olympia. Talk about battle fatigue."

Olympia chuckled, and then she shivered. "I'm not going to brush it off by saying it's all in a day's work. We both know there could have been a very different outcome."

"Don't think I don't know that. I get the heebie-jeebies just thinking about it. You know, quiet little church in rural New England, and then you have one bad-assed blizzard, and all hell breaks loose."

"Well, I got through it scared but unscathed. If the final outcome is that Emily gets help, then I consider it a job well done. It might have taken a few years off my life …"

"… but not all of them," finished Phil. "You're a brave lady, Olympia, thank you."

Olympia hung up the phone and stared out the window at the whiter-than-white landscape. So there were questions about Emily's parents' deaths. If Emily had several versions of her life story, might she also have several versions or understandings of how her parents died?

Finally, what had her intentions been the night of the blizzard? There was only one way to find out, and it most assuredly did not involve telling Frederick or Jim. When her van was fixed, and the roads passable, she would visit Emily at the facility where she was being treated and see if she could find out for herself.

Her last task of the morning was to arrange for her van to be towed to the VW place on the Cape and have the wipers fixed. Being snowbound and immobile was delightful for a little while, but for the active and restless Olympia, it was already losing its charm.

In the outer, colder part of the house, Jim and Frederick were doing a bit of male bonding as well as making forward progress on the room of her own. The electric radiator was doing its job of keeping them warm, and the room itself no longer resembled the inside of a dumpster. The trash and clutter were gone, the walls and floor were finished, and the installation of the windows would wait until a warmer day. After lunch the two would set about priming the walls, and tomorrow the three of them might go on a field trip to the paint store.

Earlier that morning Olympia had pulled an iceberg of minestrone soup out of the freezer and set it in a pot on the woodstove to heat. By lunchtime the entire house was filled with the combined scents of tomato, garlic and oregano. Even the cats were interested. It was during lunch, with the three of them seated at the kitchen table and savoring every delicious mouthful, that the phone rang. Olympia being the nearest, she went for it, and it was a good thing she did.

"Reverend Olympia? It's Eileen Sullivan."

A phone call at home was not good. Olympia was instantly concerned.

"Hello, Eileen, how are you doing in the storm? Did everybody make it through all right?"

"No, I'm afraid we didn't. I've lost the baby. I'm at Cape Cod hospital, and I know I shouldn't ask, but I really need to talk to you. Can you possibly come and see me?"

There was no question. "Of course, Eileen. The roads look pretty good. If I don't run into any trouble, I should be there within the hour."

Olympia hung up the phone and turned to the men sitting at the table.

"Jim, can I take your car? That young pregnant woman I've been working with has miscarried, and she's totally distraught. I'm going down to see her."

Jim was already pulling out his keys. "Of course, here. What a shame. When will you be back?"

Olympia did a bit of internal calculation before she answered. "Suppertime, probably. If it's going to be later, I'll let you know."

"How far along was she?" asked Frederick.

More calculation. "Eight to ten weeks, I think."

"Sad as it is, better this than have an unhealthy child. She's young. She'll no doubt have another. My mother had several miscarriages and still raised four healthy children."

Olympia put the car keys on the table and sat back down. She spoke gently.

"You're right, Frederick. The technical term is miscarriage, because the fetus wasn't viable; but Eileen made the agonizing decision to keep that baby, and now it's gone.

She may well have another, but right now she's a grieving mother and she needs someone who understands that."

Jim reached out and put his hand over Olympia's. "Be careful on the back roads, Olympia, they can be dangerous."

"Thanks, Jim, it's all main roads. I should be fine. I have to go change."

In minutes she was back, wearing a clerical shirt over dark slacks and topped with a wine colored blazer. Soon she was on the road with a mug of fresh coffee in hand, an apple and a banana on the seat beside her to make up for the soup she didn't finish, and driving Jim's nice warm car. Olympia was on a mission of mercy and compassion, and following that, she would go on to the treatment center where Emily Goodale was recuperating. The men didn't need to know that part of it. They'd only make a fuss, and she didn't feel like listening to it.

At four in the afternoon a somber-faced Olympia was back on the road. It didn't matter how many times she'd done this kind of thing; it never got any easier. She did take some small measure of comfort in knowing that the very act of showing up and whispering a prayer, of being present and being witness to the grief and the loss, was something few others could do. For the last two hours she'd sat and listened and wept and prayed with Eileen Sullivan. One day she very likely would have another child, but this was not the time to speak of it. Olympia pressed down on the gas and tried to concentrate on the road ahead. She was headed back up-Cape toward a life-care and rehabilitation facility which also housed a psychiatric care center.

When she arrived, she went to the desk, gave her name, explained she was a minister and asked if she could make a pastoral call on one of her parishioners, Emily Goodale. The woman in charge pressed a few buttons, then picked up the phone and made the request. In a few minutes a nurse came through the door and extended his hand. "Hi, I'm Jon Rice. If you'll follow me, I'll take you to see Emily. I told her you were here, and she's delighted you've come."

That evening Jim, Frederick and Olympia were putting the kitchen back in order after a particularly inventive and messy supper. The two men had gone through the 'fridge and put everything that didn't run away into a death-defying vegetarian chili that was steaming and bubbling on the back burner when Olympia returned home. Now it was payback time, and everyone was wiping down splattered countertops and washing off greasy knives and spoons.

Frederick must have had the upper hand in this project, thought Olympia. Jim was Mr. Fastidious about everything, especially cooking. Actually, chili was not something Jim would undertake of his own volition. It was far too commonplace—spell that easy. But who cared? It was delicious, it was comfort food, and the aftereffects could be hilarious, depending on how common was one's sense of humor. Olympia giggled at the thought.

"How was that poor woman who lost her baby?" asked Frederick. The three of them, plus cats, were in the sitting room.

Olympia bit her lip. "Terribly sad. She lost a lot of blood when it happened, so they're keeping her in the hospital for a couple of days just to make sure she's all right."

"Makes sense," said Jim.

"And …" She paused. At first, she hadn't planned on saying anything about visiting Emily, but then she'd thought better of it. She began again. "And I also visited Emily Goodale."

"You *what*?"

"Hold on. I checked first as to whether or not it was advisable, and they said they thought it was, so I went. It was a good visit, and it answered a lot of questions. She doesn't have any family, you know."

Frederick was trying to keep the irritation out of his voice. "I hope you aren't considering adopting her, Reverend Brown?"

"Not on your life. It was a little awkward at first, but the nurse stayed in the room with us. After a few minutes Emily seemed to relax and even said she was glad I came and apologized profusely for what happened. She said she'd stopped taking her medications shortly before I came to Salt Rock. That, coupled with a number of other contributing factors, including the five-year anniversary of her parents death, led to the fixation on me and an intensification of her delusional thinking."

"What's going to happen when she gets out?" asked Jim.

"I don't know. Probably nothing, if she stays on her meds and has someone monitoring that. I do know it won't happen until she's stabilized and has a support system in place. Worst case scenario is she starts stalking me again, and if that happens, I can get a restraining order."

Jim shook his head. "Let's hope and pray it never comes to that."

"Amen," said Olympia.

Thirty-Two

By the beginning of April, almost two months after the storm, the last traces of the snow piles were finally gone, daffodils were everywhere, and the Cape was dressed to the nines in bursts of yellow, pink and purple. Olympia had two weeks left on her temporary assignment, and she was already feeling the separation sadness that preceded the ending of a contract. She'd made some lovely friends here and to celebrate it, a group of them, spearheaded by Lynn Carver and Peggy McGrath, were planning a special Sunday brunch in her honor. But today Olympia was alone in her office, planning her last two Sundays and tying up loose ends prior to her departure. She wanted to leave a clear desk, literally and metaphorically, for Phil Rutledge when he returned, so she'd come in early to work in peace.

"Reverend?"

Olympia looked up to see Emily Goodale standing in the doorway. She was the picture of spring, clear eyed, pink cheeked and smiling.

"I saw your car in the parking lot, so I came in. I hope I'm not disturbing you."

Olympia willed herself to be calm and be what they called in seminary a non-anxious presence.

"You aren't disturbing me. Come in and sit down."

Emily limped over to the chair. She was wearing a walking cast and using a four-pronged cane. Walking and getting in and out of chairs would require skill, effort and perhaps some assistance.

"I know you are going to be finished here in two weeks, and they're planning a big brunch in your honor, but I wanted to come in and say thank you myself—alone."

"You don't have to thank me, Emily, I ..."

She waved away the rest of the sentence. "Oh, yes, I do, and I'm back on my medications, which means I'm good in my head. I want to thank you for being so kind to me, for not turning away from me because I have mental illness. You included me and made me feel like I had something to offer."

"Well, you do."

"Not everyone sees it that way, Reverend. Even my parents saw me as, well, different. When they died, because of the way they died, you know some people automatically assumed I did it. Well, I didn't, and you believed me. So you see why I wanted to say thank you just myself and not in front of a whole bunch of people. I know I made life really hard for you, but when it was all happening, I couldn't stop it. That night, I really did want to end it all for both of us. That way I couldn't bother you anymore."

"But you didn't, and we both made it through, didn't we Emily? Every day is a new beginning for both of us. I'm glad you're back."

That evening, after a companionable stroll around the neighborhood, Frederick decided to turn in early, leaving Olympia alone in the sitting room with her cats, her thoughts and Miss Winslow's diary.

April 5, 1863
In these last several months I have seen so many changes. Thanks to Aunt Louisa's loving chicanery, in the eyes of all but Richard and me I am a married

woman. Also thanks to her, I am the owner of a most comfortable home in Cambridge. And, thanks to I know not what, I shall soon be able to call myself a novelist. I have decided to use my own name from now on in the belief that women need to be recognized and acknowledged for what we do and not hide behind a male name or androgynous and anonymous initials to be deemed credible.

Before long Richard and Jonathan and I, and Sammy, of course, will spend some time in Cambridge, settling Aunt Louisa's affairs. Beyond that I cannot say. I know I will not allow myself to be restricted because I am a woman, but to do that I can no longer be silent or remain in the shadows.

Of late I have come across the writings of a woman Universalist minister by the name of Olympia Brown. She writes passionately about the need for proper and rigorous education for women and for a woman's right to vote. I want to know more of her, and perhaps, now that I am free to travel, we might even arrange a meeting.

More anon, LFW

"Well, well, well," said the Reverend Doctor Olympia Brown, "And more anon to you, too, dear lady."

Meet Author Judith Campbell

(Rev. Dr.) Judith Campbell is a Unitarian Universalist Community Minister. In addition to the Olympia Brown Mission Mysteries, she writes poetry, short stories, children's books, and articles on religious faith and the creative spirit. She offers writing workshops and retreats across the US and annually in the UK. She lives with her husband, Chris Stokes, and two thoroughly spoiled felines in Plymouth, Massachusetts, and on Martha's Vineyard. Rev. Judy loves to talk with readers and answers every e-mail personally. She is available to preach in your church and/or lead a retreat or workshop, or speak in your local library or bookstore. Just say when!

~

Author's Note: As this story unfolded I realized that it is not only #7 in my Mission Mysteries. It is also a plea for greater understanding and compassion for everyone who is coping with mental illness that affects us personally or someone we love. For more information on the subject, please go to The National Alliance on Mental Illness's website at www.nami.org.

Preview of the next title in the Olympia Brown Mystery Series, coming from Mainly Murder Press in 2015

A Premeditated Mission
by Judith Campbell

Find out how it all began in this exciting "prequel."

Up the street, across from the campground in the deserted crew dorm, a young man climbed up on top of a battered old camp dresser and tossed one end of a strip of folded sheeting over the ceiling beam. He pulled on it to test its strength and then secured it. Once that was done, he tied the other end around his neck. He had taken great care with the measurements so that when jumped and kicked the dresser away from beneath him, his feet would not reach the floor. He hoped, even dared to pray, that it would be quick.

~

A fiftieth birthday, whatever else it might be, is a milestone. It can be a warning signal, a turning point or both. The Rev. Dr. Olympia Brown was coming up on that significant event with as many questions in her mind as she had years logged on the calendar. Among them was, should she continue as a college chaplain and professor of humanities and religion at Merriweather College or leave academia and take on a full-time parish ministry?

On the nonprofessional and more personal front, there were more questions. Now that her two sons were technically out of the safe suburban nest, her status as a not-very-swinging single was becoming more and more lonely. Maybe she should be more proactive about creating a little more action in that corner of her life. Maybe she should move out of her white, middle class, three-bedroom expanded Cape in the town with the good schools and move into Boston or Cambridge. That would certainly ease her commute.

She could take her mother's advice, let nature take its course and wait for the universe to reveal what her future might hold, but Olympia rarely took her mother's advice, so she crossed that one off even before she wrote it down.

And so it was on a spectacular summer day in early June, she was sitting in her back yard, sipping iced tea and making a list or maybe a five-year plan. Olympia hadn't decided which. She created three columns across the top of the first page in big block letters: Done, Yet to Be Done, and Within the Realm of Possibility. She created a fourth section on its very own sheet of paper labelled Pipe Dreams/Pie in the Sky/Off the Chart.

Olympia Brown was methodical and well organized. She typically set reasonable goals for herself and then, in her own determined fashion, strategized how to reach them. At age almost fifty, she knew who she was and pretty much what she wanted out of life. She also knew what she was and was not prepared give up in order to bring that about, or so she thought.

Nothing that was about to happen that coming summer was on her list, and no one, not even the practical plotter, Reverend Doctor Olympia Brown, could have predicted it or planned for it. She couldn't know it, but she was at the mercy of a host of gods and goddesses who were bored and decided to have to have a bit of fun. The object of their flights of fancy and foolishness was a middle-aged, slightly restless college professor/chaplain who in one unguarded moment said she might be ready for a change.

Olympia's mother had also told her, "Be careful what you wish for." It would have been good advice had she listened, but she didn't, and therein hangs the tale.

There was no doubt she was restless. Her present academic rut was sweet and boring and far too comfortable. On the list of things she might possibly do to brighten up her life were: join a dating service for middle-aged people, take a trip, change jobs, get another cat, write the great American novel, and/or go camping for a couple of weeks. Being an academic gave her the unique advantage of having almost three months every summer to herself, supposedly for academic study and research. When her boys were younger it had allowed her to be home with them—spell that, keep an eye on them—as they stumbled through their teenage ups and downs. Now summers were lonely, and right after she wrote the words "go camping" on the possibilities list, she knew she had her answer. Not two days ago she'd received a call from the managing director of Orchard Cove, a religious campground and conference center in southern Maine, asking if she'd consider being their summer chaplain. He told her she would be responsible for Sunday morning services and a daily gathering for meditation and prayer in either the morning or evening, her choice, and be available for pastoral care if needed. Other than this, her time would be her own.

That's what they always say, she thought, twirling a pencil in her fingers, but what the heck, the timing couldn't be better, and the price was right. While they would not offer her a salary, she would have free meals and her pick of a prime spot in the campground. There she could chase off the skunks and raccoons, commune with nature, write a little poetry if she so desired, and think about what she might do for the next forty or fifty years.

It was the perfect solution. She would have time to think, no doubt about that, and she would have some really lovely people with whom she could discuss her options. Then there was the purely social side of it. The possibilities were multiple and well worth investigating. Olympia smiled at her good fortune and picked up the handset of the new portable phone she'd just purchased. She'd conveniently memorized the number.

"Hi, Brad? It's Olympia Brown. You called me a couple of days ago asking if I wanted to be the summer chaplain up there, and the answer is yes. What do I need to know, and when should I arrive?"

"That is terrific, Olympia. I was hoping you'd do it. I'll send out everything you need to know, including a map of the campground, this afternoon. You'll need to be up here by June twentieth for our staff and leadership orientation. The official season doesn't begin for another week, but there's always more to do than we anticipate, so we try and give ourselves the time. If we get lucky, we can take the last few days off for ourselves before the merry madness begins."

"Anything I should know or be aware of before I actually get in the car?"

Brad Davies paused for a nanosecond before responding. "Well, yes, no or maybe. I'll tell you and let you decide. We have a new crew boss this year. He's come up through the ranks, starting as a camper. Then he was a dishwasher, and after that he went onto the maintenance crew. He was the logical choice, but, well, let's just say he can be a little demanding. He's had some scuffles along the way. He can be a bit of a perfectionist. So while we need to get the work done around here, we want the crew to be happy and have a good time while they are doing it. Do you see what I mean?"

"I think so. Tell me more," said Olympia.

"His name is Derek Jamison. He's definitely earned his stripes along the way in terms of hands-on experience, and he has every qualification to do a good job. He's also got the life-long history of coming here year after year to go along with it. That counts for a lot at Orchard Cove. It's my job as manager to keep an eye on him, but since you'll be doing the religious and spiritual component of the orientation program, I'd like you to tell me what you think. Then, if it seems necessary, we do what needs to be done to guide and support him."

"Or let him go," said Olympia.

"Oh, I don't think it will come anywhere near being that serious. He means well, he just bears watching. Who knows, he might have totally gotten past all of it with a second year of college under his belt."

"College can work wonders with bringing on maturity. It's what I do during the year. I help young women grow up in spite of themselves." And I'm good and sick of it, she added to herself. I really do need a summer away from everything familiar, and it's been dropped right into my lap. I didn't even have to ask.

"Okay, Brad, send me the stuff, and I'll go dig around in the attic and the cellar and see what the mice have left of my camping equipment."

She hung up with the sound of his pleasant chuckle bubbling in her ear. Brad was a good man. She'd worked with him before on events and special projects in the district, and she knew him to be a person she could trust. She smiled and ruffled her fingers through her short salt and pepper hair and then stretched her arms high above her head and arched her back. It was going to be a good summer, just what the doctor, or in this case the Reverend Doctor, ordered. In September she'd go back to Merriwether and either sign another contract or write a letter of resignation effective the following June. Only time would tell which it would be.

__Coming in 2015 from Mainly Murder Press__
__www.MainlyMurderPress.com__